THE RED
SABBATH

THE RED SABBATH

**Center Point
Large Print**

ॐ श्री गणेशाय नमः

THE RED SABBATH

LEWIS B. PATTEN

CENTER POINT PUBLISHING
THORNDIKE, MAINE

This Center Point Large Print edition
is published in the year 2001 by arrangement with
Golden West Literary Agency.

The text of this Large Print edition is unabridged.
In other aspects, this book may vary from the original
edition. Printed in Thailand. Set in 16-point Plantin type
by Bill Coskrey.

ISBN 1-58547-081-3

Library of Congress Cataloging-in-Publication Data

Patten, Lewis B.
    The red Sabbath / Lewis B. Patten. -- Center Point Large Print ed.
    p. cm.
    ISBN 1-58547-081-3 (lib. bdg. : alk. paper)
    1. Little Bighorn, Battle of the, Mont., 1876-Fiction. 2. Custer, George
Armstrong, 1839-1876--Fiction 3. Large type books. I. Title.

PS3566.A79 R43 2001
813'.54--dc21

                                                      00-050912

JI

I

IT WAS COLD when I woke up that Sunday morning and my blanket felt damp from the morning dew. I laid still for a minute, listening, before I opened my eyes and looked around.

Standing against the dark gray sky at the top of the towering pile of rock the Indians call the Crow's Nest, I could see the skinny shape of the Crow scout, Hairy Moccasin. Why the Indians call that rock pile the Crow's Nest I don't know unless maybe crows once nested there.

I threw my blanket off and stood up, shivering a little because the early morning air at this elevation was cold in spite of it being late in June. Lieutenant Varnum, Custer's chief of scouts, was still asleep, snoring softly, on his back. Charlie Reynolds and Mitch Bouyer were lumped shapes against the ground. The other Crows stirred, like animals wakened by the first light to touch the sky.

I picked up my repeating Spencer carbine and

climbed toward the pinnacle. Hairy Moccasin turned his head to look at me but he didn't say anything. I took a cigar out of the pocket of my buckskin shirt, bit off the end and stuck it into my mouth. I didn't light it. I just rolled it back and forth, savoring the taste.

I couldn't see anything yet but I knew the Sioux were there. Below in the valley of the Little Big Horn was the camp we'd been looking for. Down there were the four hundred lodges we'd trailed from the Rosebud and God knew how many more.

The other Crows came climbing up now, silently, and behind them came Charlie Reynolds and Mitch Bouyer. Reynolds had his right arm in a sling because of an infected hand.

Reynolds was a quiet one, never having much to say. Bouyer had lived around Indians so long he even talked pidgin English the way they did.

We all stood there, not talking, waiting for light to sweep away the curtain of darkness lying across the land. Down below Varnum woke and I heard him call out softly. Shortly after that he came climbing to the crest. Every movement he made was stiff and he reeled like he was drunk. His eyes were red from seventy hours of scouting with no more than a few hours sleep.

He stopped beside me. He yawned and asked hoarsely, "See anything, Lorette?"

I shook my head. "They're down there though," I said. "I can feel 'em even if I can't see them yet."

From here the land dropped away steeply to the valley where the wide, looping, bends of the river were becoming visible. I stared into the valley, seeing dark splotches where timber grew along the stream, seeing something to the north. . . .

I narrowed my eyes. I finally saw what I was looking for and said, "Smoke to the north, Lieutenant. A haze of it." And kept on trying to penetrate the haze.

Hairy Moccasin, whose eyes were some sharper than mine, turned his head and said something to the other Crows in the Indian tongue. A little later the others let their breath run out as they saw it too. Reynolds said in his easygoing voice, "That's the biggest damn pony herd anybody ever saw."

Bouyer grunted, "Biggest village too. A heap too big, I'd say."

Varnum said irritably, "I'm damned if I can see

anything!"

I turned my head. I liked Varnum. I said, "You've been too many hours on scout, Lieutenant. You're half blind from lack of sleep. But they're down there right enough. Keep looking and you'll see."

Bouyer grunted, "Look for worms, Lieutenant. Them ponies millin' around look like tangled angleworms."

Varnum squinted and shook his head helplessly. He stared a few minutes more, then sat down on a nearby rock. He took a notebook from his tunic pocket and scribbled a note. He tore out the sheet and called to one of the Crows. "Take this to the general."

The Crow went back down the rocky slope. He disappeared into the trees. A few minutes later I heard his horse pushing down through the heavy brush.

I lighted my cigar and puffed comfortably as I stared toward the valley far below. Some of the Crows climbed down off the pinnacle, gathered wood and built small fires for coffee and to cook bacon and fry biscuits in the bacon grease.

Where the 7th was, smoke rose thickly, lifted by a breeze blowing upslope from the east. Hairy

Moccasin growled angrily to Varnum in the Crow tongue, "Does Long Hair think the Sioux are blind?"

Varnum shrugged and did not reply. Smoke was also thickening in the valley of the Little Big Horn. Except for its bluish color it looked like ordinary morning haze. I could still detect the movement beneath the smoke, the restless stirring of the pony herd. I stared at it uneasily, thinking that there must be ten or twelve thousand horses there. I was also thinking that Custer had sure as hell bit off a mouthful this time. This wasn't going to be another Washita.

I smelled woodsmoke and coffee and bacon and went back down to the place we'd slept last night. I packed my blanket and other stuff on my saddle, then got a tin cup of coffee and a frypan with some half cooked bacon in it and a couple of biscuits, warmed up in the grease. I sat down to eat.

Lieutenant Varnum came and squatted next to me and a Crow brought him some food. He asked, "Made any estimate as to their numbers, Miles?"

I shook my head. "That's hard to do this soon. But I'll tell you this. There's a heap more Sioux down there than the four hundred lodges we've been following. There must be ten-twelve thousand horses in that pony herd and we don't even know we saw all of it."

"That's something the general will be glad to hear."

I nodded, trying not to let my face show what I thought about the general.

I'm a pretty good-sized man, a little over six feet tall. I weigh about a hundred and eighty. My face is kind of ugly, I guess, being bony and flat-planed, with cheekbones that are a lot too prominent and a nose like a hawk's beak or maybe like an Indian's nose. My eyes are sunk back and my eyebrows are thick. My skin's as dark as any Indian's, and my hair's long enough to braid, though it wasn't braided then.

I'm not as quiet as Reynolds, but I don't gabble either. I don't get stiffed up easy, but when I do, I get real stirred up. I don't hate many men but I hated Custer. I had good reason, too.

Hating the general didn't exactly set me apart. Plenty of the men in Custer's command hated him, some with good reason, some just because they couldn't stand the man. Nick Stavola hated him because some of Nick's friends who had deserted with him back in '67 were ordered shot by Custer rather than brought back alive. Stavola escaped being shot only by pretending to be dead. Because Custer was awaiting court-martial himself, the court trying Stavola acquitted him and he was allowed to rejoin the command. If I'd been Custer, I wouldn't have wanted Stavola behind me going into a scrap with the Indians, but Custer probably never gave it a thought. He wasn't afraid of anything.

Lieutenant Payne hated Custer too. Payne had been a close friend of Major Elliot, who had been abandoned by Custer and allowed to die with nineteen other men at the Washita.

Private John Overby hated Custer, though I'd only heard him mention it once, when he was drunk. He'd been a young boy at the time of Sheridan's Shenandoah campaign during the war. He'd been living in Front Royal, Virginia. He had watched while Custer hanged two of Mosby's captured troopers, while he had four others shot, and it was little wonder Overby had scars burned in him by that experience. His father, William Overby, had been one of the troopers hanged.

I finished my bacon and mopped up the grease with the last piece of biscuit before eating it. I drained the last of the coffee in the cup. I relighted my partially smoked cigar that I had laid aside while I ate. I puffed it without even realizing I had it in my mouth.

For no reason I could understand, I suddenly felt cold. I stared into the fire, shivering. Beside me, Lieutenant Varnum asked, "What's the matter, Miles? You're shivering."

I shook my head without answering.

"Want to ride back and see how the command is coming along?"

I shrugged. "Might as well."

I got up and walked downslope until I came to the place I had picketed my horse. I pulled the stake, coiled the rope, bridled and saddled him. I mounted and turned back in the direction from which we had come yesterday.

Custer's command had probably marched all night. The general had been pretty hot to catch the Indians we'd been following. I wondered if the men in Custer's command understood why he was in such a hurry to catch up with them.

Probably not. But I understood. Custer was afraid General Crook would come marching down the Rosebud and intercept his own hurrying command. And since Crook outranked him, any glory resulting from the coming encounter with the Sioux would belong to Crook and not to him.

I also knew how badly Custer needed success in battle to stabilize his faltering career. Grant, Sherman, even Sheridan had turned against him because he was pigheaded and insubordinate. Only Terry remained his friend.

I kept my eyes peeled as I rode down the steep ravine. I knew there might be Sioux scouts anywhere.

II

IT WAS *almost* eight o'clock when I rode into the canyon camp of the 7th Cavalry. A couple of dozen fires were going, some of them sending thick columns of smoke into the air. Troopers, bearded and dusty and red-eyed, squatted around the fires, eating bacon and hard biscuits and sipping coffee from metal cups. A few glanced up at me. Most just stared numbly at the ground.

They had marched almost all night. They were

close to exhaustion. I dismounted and got myself a cup of coffee at one of the fires.

A bunch of the officers were grouped in front of Custer's tent. They dispersed and hurried to their respective commands. Almost immediately shouted orders ran through the camp. Custer himself strode back and forth, yelling shrill, impatient orders to hurry as if he was afraid the Sioux might get away.

I finished my coffee and led my horse over to where Lieutenant Payne was standing spread-legged, yelling at his troopers to fall in.

Gordon Payne was a short, red-faced man of thirty-five. He had a close-cropped head of yellow hair and wore a wide-sweeping mustache that was red-tinged like his whiskers were. His lips were chapped and his skin was red from exposure to the sun. Like Custer's, it never seemed to tan. Payne grinned ruefully at me. "Jesus, what a night! If any Sioux were within ten miles of us they sure as hell know where we are. I never heard such a racket in my life—men yelling, mess gear banging and mules braying. If the Indians weren't superstitious about fighting at night they could have cut us to pieces in that damn narrow canyon back there."

I nodded and grinned at him but I was watching Custer, striding back and forth so impatiently, trying to hasten the departure of the command. The long hair, from which the Indian names "Yellow Hair" and "Long Hair" came, was gone and his head was as short-clipped as the lieutenant's was. He and Varnum had run horse clippers over their heads in Bismarck before we left. Now, suddenly, I wondered why. Did Custer, who was usually so cocksure and confident, have a premonition of defeat? Had he cut his hair to keep from being recognized by the Indians or had he cut it so the Indians couldn't take his scalp?

Payne's troop was falling in. They formed a ragged line, ragged because of the rough terrain. The other troops were also falling in. Their sergeants bawled orders at them, swearing savagely when they were not immediately obeyed. Horses pranced and fidgeted. The men cursed sourly.

Order gradually emerged from the disorder in the camp. Lieutenant Payne and Captain Moylan rode out at the head of A Troop and I rode along with them. I hadn't reported to Custer because there wasn't anything I could add to what the Crow scout had already told him about what we'd seen.

Behind A Troop came the others, and behind the mounted troops straggled the long pack train. There were 160 mules in the train and it was a wonder their packs didn't all fall off. I never saw such a sloppily packed bunch of mules in my whole damn life.

Payne looked back at them and made an exclamation of disgust. He said, "Well, because of them at least we know there are still some Sioux around. A cracker box fell off one of the mules yesterday and when Mathey sent a couple of men back for it they found some Sioux trying to hack it open with their knives."

I looked down at the plain trail we were following. "We'll find plenty of Sioux today, Lieutenant. I wouldn't worry about that if I were you."

At the crest of a rise, I glanced around again. The six hundred troopers of the 7th filled the canyon for almost a mile. Then came the mules, followed by McDougall's B Troop forming a rear guard.

High on the slope behind us rode Custer, accompanied by his brother, Boston, and his favorite Arikara scout, Bloody Knife. When he reached the head of the column, he put his horse recklessly down the slope, sliding the animal on his haunches, leaping him over brush until he reached Moylan and Payne and me.

He saluted Moyland and Payne briefly, received their return salutes, then glanced at me. "Have you been to the Crow's Nest, Lorette?"

I nodded, meeting his impatient stare with a level one of my own. He seemed mildly irritated as he asked, "What did *you* see?"

"A lot of smoke and more damn Indian ponies than I've ever seen gathered in one place before."

"Make any estimate as to the number of Sioux?"

I shook my head. "There were at least ten or twelve thousand horses in that pony herd but the number of bucks would depend on other things. If there are only hide lodges down there, I could make a pretty good guess but if there are a lot of temporary wickiups then guessing the number of fighting men won't be an easy thing to do. There could be from three to five visiting bucks in every wickiup." I studied him. "There could turn out to be a lot more Indians than you can handle, General." General was the brevet rank that he'd held during the Civil War. He was a colonel now, but everyone called him general.

His eyes seemed to have taken on a strange

kind of glow. He rode on ahead with Boston Custer and Bloody Knife following. Moylan and Payne came next and I rode right behind Payne. Sergeant Brody and the troop straggled along in back of me.

This way, we toiled up the steep ravine. I saw that Payne's neck was red. He was staring angrily at Custer's back.

Payne was a good soldier and an experienced one. He wasn't the kind to question the order of his superiors. He certainly hadn't questioned the 1868 campaign against the Cheyenne and Kiowa. He didn't even know that the village Custer planned to attack was returning to the reservation or that it was under the Indian Agent's protection. Payne was regular army and he carried out the orders given him. He knew there were hostile Indians on the plains. Outrages against white set-tlers were committed every day. It was the Army's task to subdue the savages and he was an Army officer.

He wasn't fond of Custer. Few of the men of the 7th were. But it wasn't necessary for him to like his commanding officer.

The record of Custer's court-martial in '67 had been common knowledge among the officers and men of the command even then. Custer had been tried and convicted of a number of serious offenses, among them insubordination, deserting his command, failing to pursue Indians who had attacked his command or to recover the bodies of soldiers killed by them. He was also convicted of ordering deserters shot rather than brought back alive and of refusing medical attention to deserters wounded but not killed. As punishment he had been suspended without pay for a year.

He returned in October of 1868 to a regiment that, under General Sully, had received a series of humiliating defeats at the hands of the Indians, to a regiment whose morale was gone. In two months' time he whipped it into shape. He reorganized it, made a fighting unit of it. But he didn't endear himself to it.

On November 23, 1868, the 7th rode out to avenge its defeats at the hands of the Indians. It rode south with Custer at its head.

Major Elliot, younger than Payne whose permanent rank was still first lieutenant, commanded G, H and M Troops. Payne rode with M.

Snow was ten inches deep on the ground. It filled the air with big, sticky flakes that turned men and horses white. Eleven troops of cavalry, seven hundred men, rode out to the sound of the band playing "The Girl I Left Behind Me," muffled by the snow-filled air. Behind the mounted troops came the wagon train, fighting its way along through the deepening snow.

Scouts lost their way. The column groped blindly on to camp that night in eighteen inches of snow on the bank of Wolf Creek.

The day after, they followed the course of Wolf Creek south, and the day after that crossed to the Canadian. On Thanksgiving Day they struck a broad trail which Elliot, scouting, followed like a hound.

Now Custer left some of his wagons behind, taking only those he thought were absolutely essential. The 7th continued, the excitement of the hunt making the troopers' blood run fast. All the next day they rode, and into the following night, but at last, in moonlight, they looked down upon the wooded valley of the Washita where an Indian herd bell tinkled, where Indian dogs barked, where an Indian child cried into the night.

Lieutenant Payne was almost as old as Custer both in experience and years. He understood the colonel's eagerness to attack even if he could not approve attacking Indians that were asleep. Custer was smarting under the rebuke of the court-martial that had convicted him, smarting under a year of enforced idleness. He wanted to show his superiors that he could pacify the frontier, a task at which others before him had failed. He wanted to brighten his tarnished name, and he knew that now was the time for it.

No reconnaissance was made. Custer had not the faintest idea how many Indians were camped in the valley of the Washita. He didn't know whether they were Cheyenne or Kiowa. He didn't know whether they were hostile or peaceful. He only knew they were Indians.

He split his force into separate commands and ordered them to take positions on three sides of the sleeping Indian camp. Troops G, H and M under Major Elliot, were to attack the village from the left rear. Captain Thompson, with Troops B and F, were to attack from the right rear. Myers, with E and I, Hamilton with A and C, West with D and K and Cook with his sharpshooters were to attack the village from the front, driving the hostiles into the five troops moving upon it from the rear. Custer personally commanded the larger force.

Dawn came at last. The band struck up "Garry

Owen," the regimental song. The cavalrymen spurred their horses down the slope, yelling hoarsely in the icy morning air.

Half dressed Indians stumbled out of their hide tipis, to fall dead on the trampled snow. No distinctions were made as to age or sex. Women and children fell as they ran, to be trampled beneath the cavalry horses' hoofs. Between Elliot's command and Thompson's, a gap appeared, and through it fled a stream of terrified Indians.

Elliot, excited as a boy, yelled at Sergeant Major Kennedy to follow him. Kennedy beckoned some troopers. Standing in his stirrups, Elliot flashed a grin at Payne and yelled, "Here goes for a brevet or a coffin!"

The major, Kennedy and eighteen troopers, galloped away in pursuit of the fleeing Indians. That was the last time Payne saw any of them alive.

I stared at Lieutenant Payne's back ahead of me and beyond at Custer, dressed in buckskins and light-colored, broad-brimmed hat. Bloody Knife still rode beside Custer and a little behind. Boston Custer rode on the general's other side.

Nobody could have been blamed for Elliot's recklessness, I supposed. Nobody but Elliot himself. Inflamed by battle and success, he had ridden off on the same glory trail that many another soldier had taken long before he had been born.

The village had been captured. Scattering, retreating Indians, some half naked in the snow and bitter cold, took cover in ravines, in brush, in pockets of timber. They fought fiercely, trying to cover the escape of their women and children from the blood-crazed troops. Pocket by pocket they were killed until none were left. Wounded Indians were killed, no matter what their age or sex. A hundred and three Indian men died. No count was made of the women and children killed, but fifty-three women and children were taken prisoner.

Custer ordered the village burned, along with its supplies. A thick column of smoke rose into the still, clear air.

Elliot and his nineteen men had not returned, though Lieutenant Godfrey of K came back from rounding up the Indians' pony herd to say he had heard firing down the valley in the direction Elliot had gone.

Custer said he did not believe the firing Godfrey had heard came from Elliot and his men. He sent out small scouting parties to look for Elliot but they were afraid to venture far from the main force. They came back, saying they had found no trace.

Payne went to Custer personally. He begged the colonel to send three or four troops to look for Elliot. Custer angrily refused.

Payne still wasn't sure why he refused, why he withdrew so precipitously from the field that night after destroying the Indian village and shooting all the horses of the Indian pony herd. He was victorious and had, except for Elliot and his men, lost only one man killed.

I have my own belief. I believe that Custer was afraid—not of death but of risking his fresh-won victory. He was afraid of another setback in his career, already teetering on the precipice.

I don't know of anyone who has ever questioned Custer's physical courage. Certainly I never have. What he must have feared, then, was not death. It was defeat. It was failure.

He had needed victory desperately and it was his after the brief fight on the Washita. He simply wouldn't risk it by following after Elliot and his nineteen men.

Let them die. That was the fortune of war.

But I knew Payne would not forget the way their frozen, naked, mutilated bodies had looked, lying where the raging, hate-filled Cheyenne had left them less than two miles from the village on the Washita. Payne would never forgive Custer for refusing to go to their aid, for refusing to rescue them. He would hate Custer for that until he died.

III

UPWARD TOILED the six hundred of the 7th beneath a gray sky whose clouds effectively hid the sun. The air, which earlier had been chilly, grew hot. Dust rose from the horses' hoofs in choking clouds, hanging heavily in the defile because there was no breeze to carry it away.

Horses and mules sweated and reeked of it. Sweat soaked the troopers' shirts at armpits and down their backs. Sourly the exhausted men cursed, these men who had rested less than five hours in the last twenty-four, who must now go on anyway to satisfy Custer's battle lust.

Custer was impatient at the slowness of the march. He was impatient of each small delay, of each halt to rest the weary horses. But at last, two and a half hours after leaving the night camp in the ravine, he raised a hand. Shouts ran back along the toiling column, growing fainter with distance as they did. Troop after troop halted. Custer beckoned to me and to Bloody Knife, and the three of us rode up the steep defile toward the Crow's Nest a mile and a half farther on.

At the foot of it, Custer swung down from his horse. He climbed on foot to the top, where Lieutenant Varnum and his scouts loafed, waiting for the troopers to arrive. Bloody Knife and I followed him.

I stared past the general into the valley of the Little Big Horn The haze was thicker. No longer did it seem smoky blue. It was purple and opaque, as morning haze and mist mingled with the smoke and dust.

But I could still see that enormous pony herd milling around beneath the smoke. I could see the lift of yellowish dust here and there where a portion of the herd was on the move.

Custer was peering down, a hand raised to shield his eyes from the glare of the bright white sky. He sent one of the Crows to bring his field glasses from his saddle case. When the Crow returned, he raised the glasses to his eyes and looked again.

Mitch Bouyer repeated what he had said to Varnum earlier. "Look for worms, General Custer. Them horses are movin' underneath that haze of smoke and they look like tangled angle-worms."

Custer continued to stare. At last he lowered the glasses from his eyes. He scowled at Bouyer, at Reynolds and at me. He shifted his glance to Lieutenant Varnum. "What do *you* see down there?"

Varnum said, "Nothing, but my eyes are tired from lack of sleep. I believe Bouyer and Reynolds and Lorette, General. They've got better eyes than either you or me."

Custer shook his head angrily. "I've been on these plains a good many years and my eyesight is as good as anyone's. I can't see anything down there that looks like Indian ponies."

Bouyer said, "General, if you don't find more Indians in that valley than you ever saw before, you can string me up."

Custer glanced at him irritably. "All right, all right, all right, all right! It would do a lot of good to hang you, wouldn't it?" Turning, he went down

off the pile of rocks with swift, impatient move-
ments to his waiting horse.

Bloody Knife followed him worriedly. "Too
many Sioux there, General," he rumbled haltingly.
"It take days to kill them all."

Custer laughed with amused tolerance. "Oh, I
guess we can get through them in a day," he said.
He swung to his saddle and spurred the horse
back down the canyon toward the place where he
had left his troops earlier. Silently the Arikara
scout followed him.

Varnum was staring after Custer with admiration
in his eyes. I studied the lieutenant. I realized that
to Varnum, Custer was little short of a God. He
was familiar with every detail of Custer's military
history.

I knew a little about it myself, mostly because
few of the men in Custer's command liked him
much. But they liked to talk about him among
themselves and mostly they talked him down.

I knew how Custer had come by the sword he
carried so proudly on parade, the sword that bore
the Latin admonition, "Draw me not without
reason; sheathe me not without honor." To get it
and a handsome horse, Custer had shot a fleeing

Confederate officer in the back when it would
have been just as effective and a lot less murderous to simply shoot the horse and take the
officer prisoner.

Bouyer was staring after the general. He
turned his head and looked at Varnum. "He's
goin' after them, sure as hell."

Varnum nodded. "He sure as hell is and he'll
whip them, too."

Bouyer didn't reply. We sat there staring out
across the valley, each one of us thinking his own
private thoughts. I don't know how much time
passed, but at last we could hear the faint sounds
of the regiment stirring and rumbling into
motion. Trumpets were faint and far away. A little
chill ran down my spine.

Custer *was* going down into the valley of the
Little Big Horn. He *was* going to attack the Indian
encampment there as blindly as he had attacked
the Indian village on the Washita. He had no
intention of waiting for Terry and Gibbon, who
were marching south from the Yellowstone. Once
again he intended to ignore specific orders given
him just as he had ignored General Terry's direct
order that he scout the headwaters of Tullock
Creek and send the results of his scout to

Gibbon's column on the Big Horn south of the mouth of Tullock Creek.

The sounds of the regiment grew louder as it approached. Individual shouts were recognizable, even though their words were not. And then, suddenly, a shouted command went back along the line, repeated endlessly, and the column ground once more to a weary halt.

Men dismounted and squatted beside their horses' drooping heads. Dust settled gradually. The brassy voice of a trumpet broke the weary silence with the familiar notes of Officers' Call.

Mounted officers left their commands and climbed the steep side of the ravine to where General Custer and Boston Custer and Bloody Knife and several other Arikaras waited in the oppressive heat. Major Reno came, and Captain Benteen, and Mathey and Weir and Godfrey, Moyland, McIntosh and French, Smith, Yates, Keogh and Calhoun. Tom Custer came, as did the lieutenants from the various companies.

I climbed down off the pile of grayish rock along with Charlie Reynolds, Bouyer and Lieutenant Varnum and joined the others standing before the general.

Custer stared at us, head raised like a hound

that has suddenly caught a scent. "Gentlemen, the scouts claim to have seen a Sioux pony herd in the valley of the Little Horn, but I do not believe we will find any Indians there. I believe they have fled and I intend to follow as swiftly as possible and force them to fight. Your troops will move out as soon as they are ready. Captain Benteen, lead out with H Troop."

Benteen nodded shortly. His usually benign face was hard as he looked at Custer. I stared at him, thinking that here was another in Custer's command who bitterly hated him. Benteen had hated him for a long, long time and Custer's abandonment of Elliot at the Washita had only added fuel to Benteen's animosity.

Benteen had not, however, been as silent about it as had Lieutenant Payne. He had written a letter condemning Custer's action on the Washita to an old Civil War comrade in St. Louis. The letter had, unfortunately and without his consent, been published in the *Missouri Democrat* and had received nationwide publicity, which hadn't exactly endeared Benteen to the general.

Custer dismissed his officers. Saluting, they turned and made their way back to their respective commands.

Benteen's H Troops was near the column's head. It lurched into motion, with Benteen leading it. His eyes were hard. His face was florid, even more so than usual, from the heat. His bushy white hair was visible beneath his officer's campaign hat.

I mounted and joined him at the column's head. Over the spine of the mountain ridge we rode and began the descent into the valley of the Little Big Horn, which the Sioux call "Greasy Grass."

I could no longer see the valley floor. A ridge on the right hid it from my sight. Glancing back, I watched the long column of weary horses and men come over the brushy crest of the ridge.

I settled down comfortably in my saddle. If we couldn't convince Custer there were Sioux in the valley, then there was nothing more any of us could do.

IV

RIDING DOWN toward the broad valley of the Little Big Horn, I suddenly realized that the time had come. I had hated Custer for a long, long time and I could kill him today if I really wanted to. The opportunity would present itself. The men of the 7th were going into battle with Custer leading them.

Yet somehow the need for revenge wasn't as strong as it once had been. The intervening years had cooled the hatred I had felt toward him at first.

Besides that, I understood Custer better than I ever had before. I could see his vanity and the merciless spurs of ambition that drove him on. I could see his torment, he who could number the true friends of a lifetime on the fingers of one hand. No. Let his ambition and vanity destroy him. I no longer hated him enough.

I turned my head and looked at Benteen's face, so grim and formidable. There was something in

Benteen's expression I had not seen there before. Not fear, certainly. Uneasiness perhaps.

Benteen had been a brigadier general during the war. He also had led a brigade, but not in the headlong way that Custer had. Benteen was a better cavalry tactician than Custer would ever be, and so Benteen was probably realizing now how completely Custer was throwing away the plan for proceeding against the Sioux, the battle plan so carefully thought out before the campaign began.

General Crook was to have marched north from Fort Fetterman with ten companies of the 3rd Cavalry, five of the 2nd and six companies of the 4th and 9th Infantry. His force of over a thousand men was to have moved to the head of the Tongue River, driving the hostiles ahead of them. I didn't know where Crook and his men were now, but they appeared to have succeeded in driving the Indians north. The trail we were following had come down the Rosebud from the south.

General Gibbon had marched east from Montana, from Fort Ellis and Fort Shaw, with six companies of the 7th Infantry and four troops of the 2nd Cavalry. This force, of approximately four hundred men, along with Crow scouts, had moved down the north bank of the Yellowstone for the purpose of keeping the Sioux from escaping by crossing it.

From Fort Abraham Lincoln, near Bismarck, the eastern column moved west, twelve troops of the 7th Cavalry, under Custer, four companies of the 6th Infantry, a company of the 17th Infantry and a battery of Gatling guns with a platoon of the 20th Infantry. This force also numbered about a thousand men.

From three directions they had moved upon the Sioux, with the 7th being supplied by the steamer "Far West" on the Yellowstone. But Custer, in his greed for glory, had thrown the plan away. He was hurrying even now for fear Crook would join him and steal the glory of the victory. He had not scouted the headwaters of Tullock Creek as ordered and sent word to Gibbon advising him of the results because he did not want Gibbon any more than he wanted Crook.

This was to be Custer's victory and his alone. I knew Benteen understood that as well as I did.

From the rear came the sound of galloping hoofs. I turned my head and saw General Custer, Boston Custer and Bloody Knife overtaking us. Custer's buckskins were dusty and stained with sweat. His face was red. His light-colored, broad-brimmed hat fitted him loosely because of the fact that he had cut his hair. His manner was quick and nervous as he slowed his horse to a walk beside Benteen. The newspaper correspondent, Mark Kellog, brought along against Sherman's advice, now galloped forward to join him at the column's head.

Custer gestured toward the gray-brown, bare hills fingering into the Sundance Creek drainage from the left. "Take your troop and D and K, Captain Benteen, and scout those ridges on the left. Drive everything you encounter before you. Do you understand?"

Benteen nodded and saluted perfunctorily. The fact that he detested Custer was hard for him to hide. It was plain to me and it must have been as plain to Custer but if it was he gave no sign of it.

Custer, his brother, Mark Kellog and the Arikara, Bloody Knife, pulled aside and climbed the slope. I followed them part of the way to get out of the way of Benteen's three-troop command. His own H Troop, Weir's D Troop and Godfrey's K swung left, crossed the trickle of Sundance Creek and climbed out of the steep ravine onto the rough slopes lying to the left.

Major Reno, without specific command of his

own, galloped his horse in pursuit and flung a question at Benteen. Benteen answered him but I didn't hear his words.

Dust rose from the hoofs of the departing troopers in blinding clouds. From behind the other troops closed up. Reno returned to the column's head. He looked dejected. His rank should have entitled him to command the three troops now veering away to the left but his inexperience had no doubt prevented Custer from giving the command to him. Reno was new to the frontier. He had never been in a battle with the Indians.

Cook, Custer's huge, side-whiskered adjutant, rode his plunging horse up the slope to where Custer and the others were, no doubt returning from some errand Custer had sent him on. Custer turned his head and spoke to him in clipped sentences. Cook slid his horse past me down the slope to the column's head. He said, "Major Reno, the general directs you to take specific command of Troops M, A and G."

Reno turned a puzzled face to the adjutant. "Is that all he said?"

"That's all, sir." The adjutant saluted and returned to Custer on the slope.

Lieutenant Varnum rode forward with his scouts and beckoned me. He fanned them out ahead and to both sides of the advancing cavalry. He sent me up the steep slope to the right.

Here, twisted, stunted piñon pine and cedars grew. Sagebrush turned the dry slopes gray. I could see part of the valley ahead but the view to the north where the Sioux horse herd had been was cut off by another ridge.

Benteen's column drew steadily away. I stopped my horse and stared at the two toiling columns of cavalry. Once more, I thought, Custer was dividing his force, just as he had on the Washita. Before making a reconnaissance to find out what he was up against, he was dividing his force and weakening it.

Varnum's Crow and Arikara scouts proceeded slowly and fearfully along the ridges lying on both sides of Sundance Creek. They had more sense than Custer had, I thought. They knew the Sioux were there in the valley ahead of them and they were afraid.

I wondered suddenly if I would survive this day. I wondered if any of us would.

V

THE AIR in the descending valley of Sundance Creek was hot and humid, though the sun had still not broken through the clouds. The stink of sweating horses, of manure, of leather and of sweat-soaked uniforms was like a heavy pall mingling with the dust.

Saddle girths creaked, and stirrups sometimes clanged, and bits jangled as horses tossed their heads to shake off flies. Men cursed and grumbled. Some chewed tobacco, occasionally spitting a stream at a nearby bush. Some smoked pipes. One or two rolled dead cigars back and forth between chapped lips.

The pack train lagged, plagued by frequent stops to repack mules. McDougall's B Troop stayed with it as guards. Reno crossed over to the left bank of the stream with his three troops. Custer remained on the right with the five still under his command. Benteen and his three troops had long since disappeared.

Slouched in their saddles, the weary troopers covered a dozen miles. Varnum's scouts stayed out ahead, on ridges to right and left. I rode at the crest of the first ridge to the right of Sundance Creek. Several times it petered out as another dry watercourse joined that of Sundance Creek. Each time that happened, I climbed my horse to the crest of the new ridge appearing on the right.

The Indian trail remained on the right bank of Sundance Creek. At last, Custer waved his hat, signaling Reno to cross over with his three troops. Reno obeyed.

Suddenly I halted. On both sides of me the Indian scouts halted too. They peered nervously ahead down the valley of Sundance Creek.

A single Sioux lodge stood there, smoke flap spread. Brown, conical, it seemed deserted but the Arikara and Crow scouts continued to stare at it suspiciously.

I rode ahead and a few moments later Charlie Reynolds and Bouyer joined me. Varnum rode to the three of us, the Crows and Arikaras following reluctantly.

The trail of the four hundred lodges that we had followed all the way from the Rosebud now seemed dangerously fresh. I could almost smell the dust of their passing in the air.

We approached the lodge slowly, not sure but what it was some kind of Indian trap. No smoke drifted up from the spread flap at its top. No dogs barked at our approach.

One of the Arikaras opened the entrance flap and peered inside. He entered, beckoning the others to follow him.

I looked inside. There on a buffalo robe at one side of the fire lay a dead Indian brave, his weapons beside him, his feathered headdress on his head.

Varnum asked, "Anybody know who he is?"

Reynolds nodded. "Looks like the brother of Circling Bear. I can't remember his name. I doubt if I ever knew it."

We pulled back from the lodge. The Arikaras piled dry grass and brush against one side of it and set fire to the brush. A thick column of oily smoke rose into the still, humid air, reminding me suddenly of the smoldering lodges on the Washita.

Reynolds looked at me and grinned. "Spiteful bastards. They hate the Sioux and they wouldn't miss a chance to desecrate their dead."

I nodded, thinking that men weren't much different, Indian or white.

The long column of the command entered the little clearing with Custer riding at its head. They rode past the burning lodge, each man staring at it curiously as he went by. Reno's command followed a course parallel to Custer's and forty or fifty feet away.

Custer raised a hand and the column behind him halted, with orders going back along the line once more, repeated for each company like echoes of the original command. Reno halted his column similarly. Girard, the interpreter, rode out ahead with a few of the Crows and climbed to a little knoll. He turned in his saddle and yelled at the general, "There go your Injuns, runnin' like devils!" and pointed.

Custer spurred his tired mount. The horse climbed the knoll in great lunges. Reynolds and Bouyer and Lieutenant Varnum and I rode up the knoll after the general. The remaining Crows and Arikaras followed us.

Beyond the knoll, riding toward the river which was now clearly visible in the near distance, I saw forty or fifty Sioux warriors. They were not running like devils, as Girard had said. They were cantering their horses, heads turned to look back at us, yelping derisively.

I looked at Reynolds. "Ever see coyotes bait a trap for a dog?"

He nodded. I glanced at Custer, knowing he had heard my words and wondering if they would have any effect on him. Custer kept a pack of dogs and he must have seen the way a coyote pack will sometimes send in a bitch to lure a male dog away from a farm or ranch. The way these Indians were retreating down the valley reminded me of the way the bitch coyote runs from the dog following her, not too fast but always looking back, stopping when the dog stops, going on when he approaches again. When the foolish dog has followed her over the nearest ridge he finds the pack waiting there to tear him apart.

Custer turned to Bloody Knife. "Take your Arikaras and follow them."

Bloody Knife looked pained. He stared at Custer, then at the retreating Sioux, then at his scouts. He shook his head. "Too many Sioux. Heap too many Sioux."

Custer looked beyond him at the scouts. The Arikaras stared at the ground. They scowled. Custer said, "Maybe you had all better turn in your weapons and go home. I've got no use for scouts that are afraid to fight."

Their scowls deepened but they would not look up. I could see that Custer was furious. I wondered where Benteen was, and scanned the hills lying to the left. I couldn't see anything. God alone knew where Benteen was. Maybe miles away by now. Certainly too far away to help this command.

Custer didn't seem concerned. His eyes flashed with anger over the Arikaras' refusal to follow the derisively yelping Sioux. But his mouth had tightened with excitement and he was obviously very tense.

I felt something cold growing in my chest. Custer had started down into the valley of the Little Big Horn with nearly six hundred men but he didn't have anywhere near that many now. The mule train had lagged, along with McDougall's B Troop of forty-five men. With the train itself were seven men from each troop, or eighty-four. Benteen had veered off to the left with three troops. In all the command had been reduced by nearly two hundred and fifty men, leaving Custer with two hundred and twenty-five and Reno with about a hundred and fifteen.

I remembered that enormous pony herd we had seen from the Crow's Nest earlier. Ten or twelve thousand ponies. According to what I knew of Indians, that added up to about three or four thousand fighting men at the very least. And we didn't even know we'd seen all of the horses or that we'd estimated the number accurately. There could be twice that many fighting Sioux. There certainly weren't any less and Custer meant to attack them with his three hundred and forty men or I'd judged the look in his eyes all wrong.

Reno waited with Moylan, McIntosh and French back at the head of his three troops. The men were unusually silent now. There was little talking and no grumbling. Even the horses seemed to be unnaturally still.

Suddenly Custer sank spurs into his horse's trembling sides. He slid the horse down off the knoll and resumed his place at the head of his five troops. He raised an arm and motioned the column forward.

I thought, Jesus, he's going to do it! He's really going to do it!

At a walk, the parallel columns headed down the valley of Sundance Creek. Custer had taken the wily coyote's bait.

Reynolds and Bouyer and Girard stared at each other and at me unbelievingly. The Crows and Arikaras sat their horses on the knoll, scowling resentfully at the tongue lashing Custer had given them. Varnum's eyes glowed as he stared down at the moving column immediately below. He said, "Let's go, by God! Come on!" and galloped recklessly down off the knoll.

Reynolds followed with a shrug. Bouyer and Girard and I came next. The Crows and Arikaras followed reluctantly, grumbling to themselves in the Indian tongue. That lump of ice in my chest seemed to be spreading now. I'd been in tight spots before, but always before I'd had something to say about what happened to me. Today I was as helpless as the others were.

Custer's shrill shout, "Trot!" brought me back to the present with a jolt. The order went back along the line, repeated endlessly, and the twin columns surged ahead. No sooner had they all speeded up to the trot than the order went back, "Canter!" to be repeated similarly.

I thought that Custer must have lost his mind. The horses were as near exhaustion as the men, yet he was spending their remaining strength in a galloping pursuit of Indians who weren't even running away from him. There was nothing I could do about it though. There was nothing anyone could do.

The dust rising from the hoofs of the cavalry mounts was three times as dense as it had been before. Troopers in the rear of the columns could see no farther than the men immediately ahead of them.

But there was something immensely stirring in the sight. I could see this and feel it, in spite of my certainty that we were riding straight to disaster and to death. Guidons whipped out in the wind. Dusty, bearded faces were grim, but the eyes of the men were bright. Like a ghost column they came out of the billowing clouds of dust rising from their horses' hoofs, some yelling hoarsely, some grimly silent. . . .

Cook, Custer's huge, red-haired adjutant, was riding at his side. Custer yelled something at him and Cook veered away, crossing the narrow distance between the two columns. He ranged his horse up alongside that of Major Reno.

I was with Charlie Reynolds and Bouyer and Lieutenant Varnum and some of the Indian scouts. We were between the two columns, drawing slowly closer to their heads. I could hear Cook's roaring voice. "The Indians are about two and a half miles ahead and on the jump! Follow them as fast as you can and charge them and we will support you!"

I turned my head and glanced at Reynolds. He looked as puzzled as I felt. Custer knew Major Reno had never been in an Indian fight. Yet he was sending him ahead to attack the Sioux, who must number at least four thousand fighting men, with only a hundred and fifteen men.

I thought, "Good God, the man has lost his mind! This is suicide!" I turned my head and stared at Custer riding at the head of his five troops.

He was standing in the stirrups. He held his reins in his left hand and with his right had drawn his revolver from the holster at his side.

Suddenly his cropped hair made sense. So did his haste. I could almost hear the words Elliot had shouted at the Washita hanging in the dusty air. "Here goes for a brevet or a coffin!"

Custer had little hope of a victory today. He knew the enormous odds facing his command. But he intended to have his victory or die seeking it.

The appalling thing was the callous way he was prepared to take the three hundred and fifty men remaining in this divided command along with him.

But then Custer had never shown even the most perfunctory concern about the welfare of his men. They were only tools to him, tools for making war, for furthering his ambition, for helping him in his quest for glory, which he had pursued so relentlessly all through his life.

I swung my horse slightly left. Custer's column, on my right, slowed and fell behind. Reno kept his column galloping. If he was uncertain of himself, it didn't show.

I pulled in behind the major. I was only one man but he was going to need all the help that he could get.

VI

CAPTAIN MOYLAN and Lieutenant Payne, both with A Troop, rode a dozen yards behind Major Reno. I dropped back until I was beside Lieutenant Payne.

He was staring around at the general, who was now receding with his five troops into the cloud of dust. There was a vague expression of regret on the lieutenant's face. I knew Payne would never have tried to kill Custer in battle no matter how he hated him. He was much too good a soldier for that. But I also realized he was thinking that he would have liked to be with Custer in the coming fight instead of here with Major Reno. Like me, Payne thought the command was doomed and he wanted to see how Custer would die when the time for dying came.

I caught his eye as he turned his head. I grinned at him, and he grinned back, his teeth flashing white in contrast to his dusty, bewhiskered face. There was a rueful quality in his grin. Apparently he realized that I had read his thoughts.

He'd have been disappointed if he expected Custer to die badly though, I thought. Custer would die well. Fear of death or of being wounded had not been a part of Custer's life and it would not now be part of his death.

I shook my head irritably. I was acting like an old woman, thinking of death as if I was already dead. The battle had not even begun. The Sioux might flee as they had sometimes fled in the past. They might believe a stronger force than this was standing in reserve, prepared to attack from another direction. They might believe Custer was merely trying to drive them into the larger force.

Captain Keogh, mustached and bewhiskered, galloped out of the rising dust and joined Cook and Reno at the column's head. He had been with Mathey and the mule train but apparently had been unable to tolerate the prospect of inaction when there was fighting to be done.

On down the valley swept Major Reno's three galloping companies. A low hill came between Custer's command and Reno's. I saw Reno glance behind a couple of times afterward as though he was wondering where Custer was.

It was now about midafternoon. Ahead, the shine of the river was plainly visible though the screen of trees. And beyond, above the trees to our right, an enormous dust cloud rose. Surely Custer could also see the dust. Surely he knew it could not have been made by anything but an enormous pony herd, or by thousands of mounted warriors milling around, waiting until we would be close enough for them to annihilate.

We were still on the right bank of Sundance Creek. Suddenly now we crossed, the hoofs of the galloping horses spraying alkali water and mud high into the air. The Indian trail had crossed and Reno had followed it, perhaps out of some dim fear that the Indians would get away.

No chance of that, I thought. Before another hour had passed, we might be the ones trying to get away.

On down the left bank of the little creek we thundered. The horses were lathered now. Flecks of foam blew back from my horse's neck and stuck to my buckskin pants. The river was close, flowing deep and swift between steep banks. The Indian trail headed straight for a ford and crossed. Reno's horse plunged in first, followed by Keogh's, and mine and Cook's and shortly thereafter by those of Charlie Reynolds and Lieutenant Payne.

The overheated horses thrust their muzzles deep into the clear water of the Little Big Horn. They sucked noisily. Reno tried to pull up his horse's head by brute force, without success.

The rest of us were having no better luck. Behind us the men of Troops A, M and G crowded into the river, spreading out, each man knowing his horse would have to be allowed to drink before he would go on.

I stared beyond the ford at the towering column of dust. My chest felt as though it was filled with ice. The Sioux could slaughter us right here while our horses drank. They could overwhelm us and destroy us in minutes if there were as many of them as I thought there were.

I glanced back in the direction from which we had come. Custer's five troops were nowhere to be seen. The narrow valley of Sundance Creek was empty for as far as I could see.

Back on the riverbank the Arikara scouts had stopped. They were looking beyond us toward the towering cloud of dust, whose source was hidden and screened by the trees that lined both banks and filled the wide loops of the Little Horn. They talked in hushed tones among themselves in the Indian tongue. So noisy were the horses splashing in the water, and jangle of cavalry accouterments and the murmur of the troopers' voices that I could not make out what was being said.

Lieutenant Varnum began to yell at them. "The general was right, by God! The bunch of you had better turn in your weapons and go home. There isn't a handful of guts among the lot of you!"

They stared at him resentfully, with smoldering eyes. They kept looking beyond at the boiling cloud of yellow dust. One grunted, "Too many Sioux. Heap too many." He turned his horse and dug heels into his sides. He galloped back in the direction we had come.

A couple of others followed him. Then three more. Then two more. Then half a dozen. Varnum began yelling again. Bloody Knife raised his voice and yelled angrily at his scouts in their own tongue.

The remaining ones held, and stayed, though they looked longingly in the direction the deserting ones had gone. Bloody Knife forced them into the water, where their lathered horses began to drink.

Reno, Moylan and Payne, climbed their mounts out on the far bank, dripping, shaking as soon as they were upon level ground. Girard, Reynolds, Keogh and Cook followed and I climbed my horse out of the creek after them. We moved away from the stream bank to give the troopers room to re-form and assemble once again.

Custer, who had promised Reno support, had not appeared, and the valley of Sundance Creek lay empty to the east. To the west a wide valley stretched ahead of us for several miles, rimmed on the left by bare knolls and ridges and ravines, on the right by the timber-fringed, deep-flowing stream. The source of the dust cloud and the Indian village were hidden behind the screening trees on our right.

Follow the Indians and charge them, Custer had ordered. Reno bawled at Moylan, McIntosh and French to fall in their companies. A trumpeter blew his brassy call and the troopers' dripping horses climbed out of the river and stubbornly shook themselves before they would let their riders guide them into line.

Behind the guidons of Troops A, M and G the men formed ranks. Excited horses pranced and reared. The troopers stared ahead, over the trees, at the boiling cloud, their faces pale beneath the dust. Some of them glanced uneasily back up the valley of Sundance Creek, wondering where the general was with his five troops.

Reno looked at Moylan, nearest him. His expression was uncertain, as if he wanted to ask his captains what he should do. He had never fought Indians before, but had this been one of the battles of the war, he wouldn't even have considered going on until a thorough reconnaissance had been made. He would have sent out a patrol to scout the strength and position of the enemy. Galloping headlong up the valley as Custer had ordered went against his grain, against his training, against everything in which he believed.

Moyland, French and McIntosh stared back at him with sympathy, understanding his predicament thoroughly but knowing as well that no one could solve the problem but the major himself. At last Reno yelled, "Girard, ride up on that knoll and see what you can see."

Girard galloped away toward the nearest knoll. The horses and men of the major's command quieted, the men watching the interpreter anxiously.

Girard's horse lunged up the bare side of the knoll. Dust kicked up from his horse's hoofs. He peered in the direction of the smoke, a hand raised to shield his eyes from the white glare of the thin clouds overhead. Suddenly he wheeled his horse, slid him off the knoll on his haunches and came galloping back toward us.

He pulled the horse to a plunging halt. He looked at Reno soberly. "I saw what was making all that dust, Major. It's Indians, a goddam heap of Indians, galloping up the far bank of the stream straight toward us!"

"How many?"

Girard shrugged and spread his hands helplessly. "Hundreds. Maybe thousands."

Cook, Custer's adjutant, reined his horse toward Reno. He saluted hastily. "I'll go report to the general."

Reno nodded absently. Captain Keogh joined Cook. He said, "I'll go with him. I belong with my troop."

Again Reno nodded. There was a slight frown on his face and I felt a quick stab of sympathy for the man. Custer had promised him support but Custer was nowhere to be seen. Reno was on his own and he didn't know what to do.

He looked at me. I was the scout nearest him. "Lorette, ride over that ridge and see what's keeping him. I hesitate to attack unless I know Custer will be able to support my attack."

I nodded, wheeled my horse, and forced him into the stream. In awkward lunges, he went across and climbed out on the other side. I dug heels into his sides. He was tired from the pace we had maintained today but this was no time to pamper him. He broke into a fast trot, then into a gallop, and headed across the valley toward the nearest ridge.

I could see Cook and Keogh ahead of me, somewhat to my right. The grass was cropped close here and there were horse tracks and horse sign everywhere.

Glancing left, I saw a ragged line of Indians, perhaps two miles away, riding toward me. Behind them and above them the dust cloud boiled. Reno had asked Girard how many and Girard had shrugged and spread his hands helplessly unable to estimate with any accuracy. I understood why now that I had seen them myself. How do you count a multitude whose front rank only is visible?

I drummed my heels on my horse's sides, forcing him to an even greater speed. I slashed his rump with the ends of the reins. He laid back his ears resentfully, but he dug in and ran.

Leaping small washouts and rocks and clumps of brush, he lunged up the slope of the nearest ridge. Suddenly I saw a file of horses, just beyond the ridge's crest, gray horses, those of Captain Yates's F Troop, ridden by blue-clad cavalrymen. I saw a figure in buckskins that looked like Custer appear briefly and wave his hat in the direction of Reno and his three companies.

Damn him! I thought angrily, He hasn't got any intention of supporting Reno in his charge. He's swung off to the right to attack 'em from the other side.

The appalling arrogance of the man staggered

me. With two hundred and twenty-five men in his five troops, with little more than a hundred in Reno's command, he meant to surround, attack and annihilate three or four thousand fighting Sioux. Arrogant? Hell, he was insane. Or he was deliberately trying to commit suicide.

I continued on to the crest of the ridge, though I knew I was too late. Custer would not now return to support Major Reno's charge. He had changed his battle plan without bothering to inform Reno what he had done. I had my orders, though, and I meant to carry them out.

I reached the crest of the ridge. I stared across the rolling land ahead of me.

Custer's five troops made a snakelike column half a mile long. They were at a gallop, heading straight toward the Sioux villages, the nearest tipis of which I could plainly see from here. I saw no movement, no life in the villages. I knew Custer could not see the approaching wave of Sioux Indian braves.

I remember telling myself that I had to get back as quickly as possible. I had seen where Custer was. But for an instant I couldn't move.

The air was filled with sound, as strange a sound as I had ever heard. It was not a hum exactly. It was more like a muffled roar. It was the blending of a thousand separate sounds made by thousands of separate animals and men. It was the distant pound of ten thousand hoofs drumming against the trembling ground, communicated to me as much through the ground as through the air. It was the shrill, barking cries of thousands of Indians. It was the rattle of metal against metal, the blend of the troopers' voices, the wind sighing out of the west, the murmur of the stream below.

Custer's five troops were strung out raggedly. I could see the buckskin clad figure of the general riding recklessly at their head, straight toward the Indian village. His white hat stood out plainly in the dazzling light of the afternoon.

I turned and galloped back in the direction I had come. Custer was either expecting another Washita or he was deliberately throwing away his own life and those of his men so that his name might become immortal in history.

Down off the slope I rode as fast I could force my tired horse to run. The wave of Indians was closer now, but it was still nearly a mile away. They would strike Custer's column on the left flank and Custer probably wouldn't even know what had hit him until it was too late. It would be over in minutes unless something turned that wave of Indians back . . .

From the river ford, Reno's voice came to me clearly on the light afternoon breeze. "Left into line! Guide center! Gallop!"

Like a great fan the column spread, fours to the left. The line undulated as it galloped forward, like a flight of ducks against the sky. The guide was center, the guidons there, and gradually the line stiffened and straightened and went on ahead. A Troop and M were the front line of attack, with Varnum and Bloody Knife and the remaining Arikaras and Crow scouts guarding the left end of the line.

From my higher elevation I could see what Reno could not see. Out of the horde of feathered warriors on my side of the river, fragments had spilled off, had plunged across the river and filled the plain beyond a looping river bend.

Half a dozen years ago I would have stopped my horse and stared down, gloating that the hated Custer and his men were about to be annihilated. But too much had intervened. Too much lay between half a dozen years ago and now. No longer was the issue as clear cut as it once had been.

I did not stop. I yanked my carbine from the saddle boot and belabored my horse's rump, trying to force from him just a little more speed. Leaping narrow washouts and clumps of brush, he thundered toward the ford.

Reno was already a quarter mile ahead of me. My horse hit the water and, tripped by its resistance, somersaulted into it, throwing me clear.

I came to the surface, still holding the reins. The horse was already on his feet. I mounted and kneed him out of the stream and kicked him into a gallop once again.

Slowly I began to overtake Troop G, riding in reserve. I figured Custer was finished and Reno's three troops were probably finished too, but I had to do as much as I could.

Reno's galloping, grim line rounded the bend in the river, beyond which I had seen the Sioux filling the plain on its left bank. For the first time Reno saw what was facing him.

The line faltered and slowed without command. I began to gain rapidly. I rounded the bend less than fifty yards behind Troop G, and saw what Reno had seen only minutes earlier.

The column of dust was like the smoke from a monstrous prairie fire, boiling, yellow. Beneath it was a savage horde, yelling, barbaric in their feathers and brilliant paint, firing into the air out of sheer exuberance, coming on hungry for the vengeance due them for fifty years of broken promises, for half a hundred savage massacres.

Reno glanced back once more, looking for Custer's five troops and the general's promised support. Instead he saw me, coming on alone.

On the left flank, the Indian scouts wheeled away, galloping back and to the left, deserting, leaving of all their number only Bloody Knife.

Reno flung up an arm and dragged his plunging horse to a trembling stop. "Halt!" he roared. "Prepare to fight on foot!"

For an instant all was confusion. One young trooper's horse would not halt and bolted out of control, past Reno and his captains, on into the boiling dust and howling Sioux. He was still in his saddle when he disappeared.

I swung from my horse and handed the reins to a grizzled corporal, designated a horse holder for Troop G. I headed into the milling troopers toward the place I had seen Major Reno last.

VII

These were grim, efficient troopers, these men of the 7th Cavalry. For several minutes all seemed to be confusion as they surrendered their mounts to the horse holders, who were to retreat with them to the shelter of the nearest timber along the river bank.

But out of confusion came order. Each of the horse holders galloped four horses to safety. Each of the dismounted troopers moved forward purposefully into line.

There was not a one of them who did not now know exactly what the command was up against. They were alone. They knew that Custer would not come to give them the support he had promised them. They knew they faced thousands of bloodthirsty Sioux and that very probably all of them were going to die.

But this was the moment toward which a soldier's whole life points. This was the moment of battle, for which he has been trained through all the deadly, boring days and nights.

The galloping line of Indians was now no more than a couple of hundred yards away. They veered from headlong impact, firing their rifles and arrows at the thin, wavering line of grim-faced troopers on the ground.

Reno bawled, "Fire at will!" and gunfire crackled along the line. Some of the troopers knelt to steady their aim. Some fire standing up. I wondered as I watched them reload after every shot why they did not still have the repeating Spencers they had carried at the Washita instead of the single-shot Springfields they carried now.

The stubborn line of troopers plodded forward into the hail of feathered arrows and lead. They advanced a hundred yards, step by step, literally inch by inch.

Suddenly the breeze strengthened, for an instant stirring the dust, carrying it away and lifting it. The line of grimy men stopped and stared, appalled, at what the lifting cloud revealed.

The valley was filled with mounted, feathered Indians. Five hundred, a thousand of them milled in the area separating the troopers from the Indian villages which had become visible in the distance. The line stopped as suddenly as if it had run headlong into a wall.

Rifles were heating up. Some of them had jammed. Frantic troopers were trying to pry out spent cartridges with their knives.

My Spencer was empty, its barrel hot, although I scarcely remember firing it. Several men were already dead. Several more were wounded, being helped toward the timber where the horse holders were.

A trooper came running to Reno, shouting that the Sioux were crossing the Little Big Horn behind the command, trying to get at the horses.

Reno looked around frantically, toward the rear from which direction Custer was supposed to come, toward the timber, where the horses and horse holders were. He roared at McIntosh to withdraw G Troop into the timber as a guard for them. Lieutenant Wallace bawled at Billy Jackson, a half-breed scout, to go back and hurry Custer up. Jackson looked back toward the fork and beyond up the valley of Sundance Creek. Indians, working around the left flank of the command, already were between it and the ford. He looked at Wallace and shook his head. "It's too late!" he shouted. "Nobody could get through that!"

I ran forward. I reached Reno, still stubbornly

holding his position against an overwhelming number of Indians. I roared, "He isn't coming, Major! Custer and his command bore right and they're on the other side of that ridge over there."

"How do you know he isn't coming? How do you know? He promised me support!"

"He's got trouble of his own! He's got more Sioux to fight than we have!"

At last, I thought sourly, Custer had found enough Indians, even for one as bloodthirsty as he. He had told Bloody Knife he thought he could get through them in a day. Well now let him try. Let him fight against the same kind of odds the Cheyenne had fought against on the Washita. Let him feel the way Major Elliot had, surrounded, outnumbered, doomed.

Reno must be thinking of Elliot. He must be remembering that Custer had not supported Elliot at the Washita. His face was pale beneath its heavy covering of dust and grime. His eyes, though steady, had a touch of panic in their depths.

I felt sorry for the man. He was a good officer, if inexperienced with fighting Indians. He stared at the Indians ahead, at those closing in on the left flank from which the Arikara scouts had fled, at those closing the line of retreat to the river ford. He had but one choice, to retreat into the doubtful safety of the timber on his right where the river guarded his flank, where G Troop and the horse holders already were.

Pistol in hand, he waved toward the timber. "Withdraw into the trees!"

The shout was taken up by officers and non-coms. Fighting as they retreated, the troopers backed toward the right, toward the line of trees and brush.

A man beside me was hit. He fell against me, his throat spurting blood. It drenched my hands, drenched the front of me as I caught him and supported him. He was gurgling, trying to speak, but choking on his own gushing blood. Half dragging him, half carrying him, I staggered toward shelter a hundred yards away. Reaching it, I put him down with his back against a tree and turned to shout for a surgeon. The shout died in my throat. The man was already dead.

I wiped my bloody hands on the sides of my pants so that I could operate my gun. I stood behind the tree, resting my rifle against its trunk, drawing a careful bead each time I shot.

I killed five with the remaining five shots in my

gun. I knelt and reloaded hastily. Troopers continued to stream past me. The dust boiled on the
open plain and Sioux warriors milled and
screeched like painted devils gone berserk.

We were on a kind of shallow peninsula formed
by a loop of river around the grove of trees. The
river was on three sides of us. Great cottonwoods
towered above us and beneath them was heavy
brush and smaller trees. It was a veritable thicket,
but a lifesaver for Reno's three companies. It
would give the men time to get their breath, to
regroup and reload. It would give Reno and his
officers time to assess their situation and decide
what they should do.

I couldn't see that they had much choice. They
were surrounded by the Sioux. To attack would be
suicide. To remain in this grove of trees would be
almost as bad. The only alternative remaining was
to cross the river and fight across the valley floor
to the bluff beyond. If Reno could reach a position
on the heights he would have a chance to repulse
the Indians. He might also have a chance to reach
Custer and his five companies and join up with
them.

The command was in the thicket now. Officers
shouted helplessly, unable to see their men.

Horses, terrified by the noise, some of them wounded, plunged and nickered, trying to get away from the stubborn horse holders.

My hands still bloody, I began to work my way through the thicket. I wanted to find Reno and see if there was anything I could do. There was no longer any chance of getting a courier out, either to try and reach Benteen, or to try and reach the general. We were completely surrounded by howling, exulting Indians. They screeched like maniacs. They fired blindly into the thicket with their ancient smoothbore guns. A veritable rain of arrows fell, some striking horses, some wounding men, some sticking in the trees with an odd, thwacking sound that, once heard, can never be quite forgotten by any man.

I almost bumped into Lieutenant Payne, trying to rally and gather his men. He had about a dozen and was herding them back toward the edge of the timber to form a perimeter of defense. One lanky, sandy-haired trooper drawled, "Hell, Lootenant, we're damn near out of ammunition."

"Then make every bullet count!" Payne snapped at him. He glanced up and saw me. He said, "Custer?"

I jerked my head toward the bluffs across the

Little Horn. "He was up there, last I saw of him, heading straight toward the villages."

"Then he's probably in as much trouble as we are."

I nodded. "Or more."

There was no triumph in Payne's face and I could see that he was thinking, not of Custer whom he hated, but of the five companies of men under Custer's command. I went on, still looking for Reno. Smoke was beginning to drift through the thicket from fires the Sioux had started in the dead sticks and brush deposited by the river on the upstream side of it. There was no danger of the trees and underbrush catching, but the smoke might further terrify the horses and make them even less manageable than they already were.

At all costs, the horses must be held. They would give us mobility for the dash to the bluff. Without them we were doomed.

I could hear them plunging and nickering in the depths of the thicket and scrambled toward the sound. Weary troopers were everywhere, some leaning against trees to catch their breath, some reloading with shaking hands, some drinking from canteens, some just staring hopelessly into space. The command was demoralized. It was exhausted. It had been beaten by Indians it was supposed to have been able to defeat easily.

Suddenly I saw Reno ahead of me talking to Moyland and French. His face was harried, his eyes desperate. Bloody Knife stood behind him, his swarthy face showing nothing but stolid acceptance of what was happening.

I crawled over the huge white trunk of a down cottonwood. "Anything I can do, Major?"

He looked at me a moment, apparently without seeing me. I repeated, "Major, is there anything I can do?"

"Do you think you could get through that mob of howling savages?"

I stared at him. I knew we were going to die and it probably didn't matter if I died a little sooner than the rest. I said, "I can try. But there's no use trying to reach the general again. He isn't coming to your support. He and his men are either dead or they're miles away by now."

"I was thinking of Benteen. He's up there somewhere with three fresh troops. If he could reach us we might have a chance."

I nodded. "I'll try and get to him."

Bloody Knife stared at me as if he thought I had lost my mind. Reno looked at me gratefully. I turned away and hurried on toward the horses. It took me a few minutes to find the corporal who had taken mine. I took the reins and led the horse toward the edge of the grove of trees.

At the upstream edge the Indians seemed to be less numerous than on the other side and across the Little Horn. I stood there for a few minutes, staring out across the valley toward the dun-colored line of bluffs. I was crazy for doing this, I thought. The minute I galloped out of the trees they'd be after me. My only hope was that my horse was both faster and fresher than theirs. At least he'd had a few minutes' rest. The Indian ponies had been steadily galloping back and forth ever since we appeared and maybe even before we appeared.

Crazy or not, I had volunteered to do it and it was too late to back out now. I stuck a foot into a stirrup and swung to the saddle, at the same time whacking the horse's rump with the barrel of my Spencer carbine. He broke into a gallop and I guided him toward a gap in the milling horde of howling Indians.

I swung off the horse's back, clinging to one side with only part of an arm and one foot visible to the Indians on the downstream side. They couldn't see enough of me at which to shoot. Those on the upstream side banged away but they didn't hit anything. It's hard to shoot with any accuracy from a running horse. It's harder if your target's moving too.

I think I held my breath all the way between the grove of trees and the foot of the bluff. I don't remember taking a breath and I was gasping for air when the horse started to lunge frantically up the slope. I swung back into the saddle and turned to look behind.

Three Indians were very close, already starting up the slope. I raised the Spencer and put a bullet into the horse nearest me. He fell, tripping the one immediately behind. The two horses and their riders went down in a kicking pile.

The third came on. I fired a second time, missed and fired again. The Sioux was driven backward off his horse and the animal veered aside and slid back down to the valley floor.

I was clear for the moment, I thought, and I began to breathe again. A few other Sioux were climbing the slope behind me but they were a hundred yards back and out of effective rifle range. I leaned low over my horse's neck so as to give them as small a target as possible and put my mind on getting away from them. I had no way of knowing where Captain Benteen was. There was a good chance I'd never find him at all. If I didn't, Reno's men would all be dead before I could get back to them.

Low mounded hills and bluffs through which I was traveling made this a veritable badlands of dry, dusty, ground, of low scrub brush, of deep-cut gullies and ravines. I climbed for a couple of miles without crossing any trails but a few scattered Indian trails. Reaching a high point from which I could look ahead, and finding the land completely empty, I was forced to the con-clusion that Benteen had not come this far. This was rough country and he must have had to drop into and climb out of half a hundred deep ravines. Doing so had slowed him so that he was well behind when Custer's and Reno's commands reached the valley floor.

I turned back toward the east, forcing my horse to maintain a gallop wherever possible. I might kill him but time was one thing I didn't have. Minutes might mean the difference between staying alive and being slaughtered for the men of Reno's besieged command.

VIII

FROM HIGH on the slope above the trickle of Sundance Creek, I saw the column of oily smoke still rising thinly from the smoldering tipi the Arikaras had fired earlier in the afternoon. I still had not crossed Benteen's trail and I was beginning to wonder if I had not come too far north and missed him altogether.

I did not, however, change my course. It was too late to go off on a wild goose chase farther south. If Benteen had taken his three troops south he was beyond my reach. By the time I could find him and bring him to Reno's assistance, it would be too late.

But even if I did not find Benteen, there was help to be had for Reno, coming down the valley of Sundance Creek. Mathey was escorting the pack train and should have almost reached the burning tipi by now. Behind him, as rear guard, was McDougall with Troop B. In all, Mathey and

McDougall had about a hundred and thirty men, more than were with Benteen.

I therefore veered left, but stayed high on the ridge south of Sundance Creek in order to see farther up its twisting course. Abreast of the smoldering tipi, I caught a glimpse of what looked like a cloud of dust.

I kicked my horse into a gallop again. The dust became more plain, lying heavy in the air on the south side of Sundance Creek. Coming over a low ridge I suddenly saw Benteen's three troops ahead of me, strung out along both sides of Sundance Creek where it widened to form a stagnant pool. Their horses were drinking, the men slouched in their saddles wearily and dispiritedly. It was obvious they had not heard the gunfire in the valley of the Little Big Horn. It was obvious they did not know that Custer and Reno had engaged the Sioux.

As I slid my horse down the steep slope toward them, all faces turned toward me expectantly. I rode to Benteen and hauled my horse to a halt. I said, "Major Reno sent me, Captain Benteen. He is surrounded by Sioux and badly in need of support."

"What about Custer?" Benteen gave me no

time to reply. He turned and roared an order at his command, then led out down the creek at a brisk trot, his men straggling along behind at a similar pace. I ranged alongside of him and he shouted again, "What about Custer?"

"He ordered Reno to charge the Sioux and said he would support the charge. He never did. I don't know where he is now but the last I saw of him he was attacking the village from the other side."

"How big a village?"

"Big. Too big for two hundred men to attack. Too big for two thousand men."

We were passing the burning tipi now. Glancing behind, I saw the first of the pack mules streaming into the small clearing we had left so recently. Benteen saw them too and roared at me, "Go back there and get yourself a fresh horse. Then ride ahead and inform Reno we are on our way."

I whirled my horse and rode back. I stopped the first trooper I encountered who was with the pack train and told him I had to have his horse. I changed saddles swiftly, then swung to the horse's back and rode away. Galloping, I began to overtake Benteen's command almost at once, passing them before they had gone a mile and riding on ahead down the valley of Sundance Creek.

Shortly afterward I began to hear the distant sound of gunfire. Obviously then, the men of Reno's command were still holding on. Benteen was not too late.

I encountered Custer's trumpeter, riding toward me up the creek. He yelled at me, asking if I had seen Benteen, and I turned to point. He pounded on. I supposed he had a message from Custer for Benteen, which meant that Custer's command was still intact somewhere, perhaps having found cover as Reno's had.

Short of the ford where Reno's three troops had crossed earlier, I met Half Yellow Face, the Crow scout, driving some captured Sioux ponies. He grinned at me triumphantly as though the feat of capturing horses from the Sioux at a time like this, under the very noses of thousands of them, was the greatest thing anyone had ever done. Apparently it didn't trouble him that Reno was pinned down in the timber with his dying command. It didn't trouble him that other Crows were dying with Custer in the hills north of the Little Horn.

I went on and splashed across the ford, wondering how the hell I was going to get to Reno through the horde of Indians surrounding him.

Perhaps, I thought, since I was coming from this direction they would mistake me for a Sioux. Certainly my hair was long enough and plenty of them were riding captured cavalry horses, so the horse shouldn't give me away.

Staying close to the river I rode openly toward the grove where Reno was. A few moments later I was in the middle of a swarm of Indians. All were yelling and waving their guns above their heads. I began to yell too and to wave my own rifle, and this way I got to within a couple of hundred yards of the thicket where Reno was.

My new predicament was as dangerous as riding into the swarm of Indians had been earlier. I now had to ride toward the thicket without being shot by Reno's men. To make matters worse, the minute I identified myself to Reno's men, the Sioux would begin shooting at me from behind.

A young Sioux ended my hesitation by howling that I was an enemy and taking a swipe at me with his tomahawk. I slammed my rifle barrel down on my horse's rump, dug my heels into his sides, and let go a high yell almost in his ear.

He leaped forward, slamming against a Sioux

horse and nearly knocking the animal off his feet.
Then he was running and behind me the yells of
the Indians grew more shrill and excited, like the
yapping of a coyote pack close on the heels of a
rabbit near exhaustion from the chase.

A bullet burned along my ribs, bringing an
instant rush of blood. An arrow tore through the
muscles of my left arm. Looking down, I could see
the bloody arrowhead protruding in the front.

I hung onto the horse's reins with my numbed
left hand even though I couldn't feel with it any
more. I raised my right hand with the rifle in it
and roared toward the grove, "Don't shoot me,
boys! It's Miles Lorette!"

Then I was in the thicket, tumbling from my
horse, yelling at the nearest man, "Where's the
Major? Benteen's on the way!"

The trooper gestured vaguely toward the
center of the thicket. I dragged my horse along,
feeling nausea mounting in me from the wound in
my side and from the arrow in my arm. I shouted,
"Major! Major Reno!" but there was too much
confusion in the thicket, too much noise. I got no
reply.

Ahead of me, I heard yelling and shortly afterward came to a place where timber and brush was

thinner than elsewhere in the grove. I saw Reno, pistol in hand, and I saw half a hundred troopers falling in. I yelled at Reno, but he didn't hear.

Troop A was forming at the head of the column of fours. Behind A Troop was what was left of G and in the rear was M Troop. I thought, "God, they're not all here! Why doesn't he have the trumpeter blow Boots and Saddles so they all can hear?"

Maybe he didn't have a trumpeter. Maybe all the trumpeters were dead. Suddenly Reno waved his revolver and shouted, and the column swept out of the thicket at a gallop, troopers leaning low in their saddles to present smaller targets to the Sioux. An Indian bullet split Bloody Knife's skull and blood from it splattered Major Reno's face, already white with shock.

I supposed the others would hear the commotion and bring up the rear. I tried to hold my terrified horse still long enough to mount, not an easy task with a numb left arm that had no strength in it.

I made it to my horse's back. I caught a glimpse of Lieutenant Varnum riding out of the thicket. I was near the rear of the column as it streamed out onto the valley floor. I beat my horse savagely, trying to reach Reno at the column's head so I could give him my report.

The river was on the column's left. The howling, painted Sioux braves gave before the head of it, then ranged along the right flank just out of effective range. Troopers fired recklessly and then, when their guns were empty, went down with their skulls split open as the Sioux rode in and struck them down.

I saw Lieutenant McIntosh fall from his saddle and be trampled under the following horses' hoofs. Most of the troopers' guns were empty by now and it was impossible for them to reload. They used the carbines as clubs against the Sioux when they rode close enough. Harried, doomed and well knowing it, the column swept away from the grove toward God knew where.

Varnum spurred his horse savagely to the column's head. I heard him roar, "For God's sake, boys, don't run. Don't let them whip us this way!"

Reno yelled sharply at him, "I am in command here, sir!"

I shouted at Reno, trying to make him hear, trying to tell him that Benteen was on the way. There was blood on Reno's face, and flecks of something that might have been pieces of Bloody

Knife's shattered brain. The man's face was gray. I knew he had fought in the war, and with distinction, but he had never encountered anything like this.

Back near the rear of the column the pressure from the Sioux was terrible. They closed in behind the command, like a solid rank of hungry wolves. They fired point-blank at the troopers bringing up the rear and the terrified troopers crowded those ahead, trying to escape. But there was no escape. Ahead, to the right and in the rear was a solid wall of screeching Indians. Horses fell, throwing the troopers riding them clear to be overwhelmed and killed before they could get to their feet. Gradually the pressure of the Indians forced the column left toward the river bank, at this spot precipitous and steep.

The way was closed to the ford by which Reno's command had entered the valley earlier. It was closed by a solid wall of Indians. Unceasing pressure forced the head of the column against the river's edge.

The bank here was five feet high on the right side, eight feet high on the other side. The stream ran belly deep on a horse, and twenty-five feet wide.

Hatless, his face bloody, his eyes wild, Reno

jumped his horse into the stream and the column followed him. There was no rear guard action to protect the crossing men. The retreat had become a rout.

The water boiled with horses and with men. Horses went down, killed as they fought their way across. A trooper lay face down in the water, half submerged, a red stain spreading from a deep wound in his neck. Geysers of water shot upward where bullets struck. The shrill nickering of the horses mingled with sounds of splashing animals and men, with shouts and cries of pain.

It was a trap from which there was no escape. No escape route save for one precipitous fissure leading out of the river on the east side of it, a fissure through which only one horse could climb out of at a time.

Men and horses fought to be next out of the stream. I still had not jumped my horse into it, not wanting to be trapped there, unable to fight, equally unable to escape.

But the pressure of the Sioux on the west bank gave me no choice. Only a handful of troopers remained on this side with me, and the Sioux were closing in, their howling pitched to a higher note.

. . .

I whacked my horse on the rump with my carbine and forced him to take the jump. He narrowly missed landing on another horse, whose rider dragged in the water, his foot caught in the stirrup, dead. I turned in the saddle and began firing at Indians who appeared above me on the bank.

Reno was demoralized, as were some of his officers. Panic had seized many of the men, particularly recruits who had not fought Indians before. And panic is contagious.

Reno climbed his horse out of the river, out on the far side of it. There was now a handkerchief tied around his head to keep blood from running down into his eyes. Shouting, waving his revolver, he rode back and forth, trying to reorganize what was left of his command. Indians on the west bank continued to pour withering fire from rifles and bows into the melee in the water. Indians on the bluffs guarding the east bank poured arrow and bullets down into the troopers as they scrambled out of the river by that one narrow route, their horses lunging awkwardly because of the steepness and slickness of the ground.

Dr. De Wolf was killed. Reno's adjutant, Lieutenant Hodgson, already wounded, was shot through the head as he reached the east bank, clinging to a trooper's horse.

I wondered how many were left in the grove to fend for themselves. Looking around I missed Charlie Reynolds and the Negro interpreter, Isaiah Dorman. I did not see Lieutenant DeRudio of A Troop, or Herendeen, but any or all of these might have been killed during the retreat from the grove. Or they might still be there.

But a handful now remained in the river, these waiting their turn to climb their horses out. I rode out last, just as a trooper yelled, "Look! It's Benteen!"

At full gallop Benteen's three troops came through the hills along the eastern bank of the Little Horn. His trumpeter blew the charge, the notes clear, sweeter in that moment than any sound I have heard in my life before or since.

Soaked, bloody, beaten men cheered raggedly, while in the river corpses of men killed there floated slowly downstream and out of sight.

A calm, unexcited Benteen wasted no time in taking charge. He could see how demoralized were Reno and his officers. He bawled at his men to share their ammunition with the exhausted remnants of Reno's three troop command.

A few men rode back down into the river to recover loose horses there. They brought out six or eight.

By this time, I was nearly blind with pain from the arrow, still sticking through the muscles of my arm. At every movement it sent knives of pain up into my shoulder and neck and all the way down to my fingertips. I knew I couldn't continue with the arrow in there very long. Besides, I was weak from loss of blood. My whole side was soaked with it.

Dr. Porter, the assistant surgeon, was hastily treating the most severely wounded of Reno's men on the ground. I rode to him and dismounted, if you could call it that. I literally fell off my horse. I said, "Can you get this damned thing out of here?"

He nodded and I sat down on a rock. He said, "It'll hurt."

I said, "It already hurts."

He got hold of the arrowhead end and with a quick movement broke the shaft. I felt myself falling and heard his sharp command, "Grab him, Trooper, and hold him up!"

Hands steadied me as I fought for consciousness. The surgeon seized the feathered end of the shaft in back and yanked it from the wound.

I fought grimly for consciousness. I remembered being afraid that if I lost consciousness they might think I was dead and leave me here. I tried to say I was all right but I suppose nothing more than a mumble came out of me. Dr. Porter held something under my nose, something with a penetrating smell that cleared my head and made me draw away. He was saying, "Can you ride, Lorette? Can you ride if someone helps you up?"

I nodded, then stopped and held my head still because of the pain the movement caused. The doctor was hastily bandaging the arrow wound. He had not apparently, noticed my blood-soaked side and I didn't point it out to him. I'd had enough for now.

A couple of troopers helped me to my feet and boosted me on my horse. I sat there swaying, clinging to the saddle, not caring whether some Sioux put a bullet into me or not.

Benteen's unemotional shout started the movement from the valley floor to higher ground on the east. Accompanied by Benteen's three troops, the shattered remnants of Reno's command withdrew from the field. I vaguely wondered where Custer was and hoped, God help me, that he was dead. He sure as hell deserved to die for leading us into this.

IX

MY MEMORY of the next half hour or so is unclear. I stayed upright in my saddle and rode without help, but I was near unconsciousness. The Sioux continued to fire at us, though many of them seemed to have withdrawn down the valley.

It was possible that Custer and his five troops were cornered down there someplace, also fighting overwhelming numbers of Sioux, and I couldn't help but remember Custer's unconcerned reply to Bloody Knife earlier, "Oh, I think we can get through them in a day all right."

My thoughts wandered during that ride from the river to the knoll where Benteen decided to dig in. All around me men were cursing Custer, not even bothering to keep their voices down. They weren't reprimanded by their officers, a good many of whom probably felt the way they did.

My skin felt flushed. Only half conscious, I was remembering things that had happened a long, long time ago.

Westport, Missouri, was where I was born and raised. My pa skippered a steamboat that ran between Westport and St. Louis.

I got acquainted with young Charles Bent in Westport when I was twelve. He was the son of William Bent, one of the founders of Bent's Fort on the Arkansas, and of Owl Woman, his Cheyenne wife, who died when Charles was born. Charles's pa was afraid he'd turn out more Indian than white, so he sent him East to school.

In 1861, when the War between the States broke out, Charles left school and enlisted in the Confederate Army, lying about his age. I tried to enlist but was refused, probably because I didn't look as old as Charles. Two years later, though, they found out how old he really was and discharged him. He came through Westport on his way home to Colorado and Bent's Fort. He persuaded me to go with him, which wasn't hard because by then I was all alone. My pa had been killed by a drunken stevedore six months before and I sure wasn't too fond of the job I had loading freight on the river front.

The two of us traveled west on horses Bent bought with money he'd earned in the army, sometimes in the company of a wagon train, sometimes just the two of us alone. When we arrived at Bent's Fort Charles's pa was gone, so we left right away and went out looking for the Cheyenne villages.

Both of us had let our hair grow long. We'd gotten Indian clothes at the fort and we looked like a couple of Indian bucks. When we reached the village where Owl Woman's relatives were, they welcomed us like we were part of the family, which Charles was even if I was not.

I'd been scared of Indians all my life, having heard only the wild stories the trappers in Westport told. Now I began to find out what friendly, decent people they really were. The two of us lived in the lodge of Two Horses, a middle-aged brother of Owl Woman, along with his two wives and three sons, who were first cousins to Charles. He gave me a horse of my own, a rusty old rifle, and a bow and some arrows. He also gave me a knife and a tomahawk.

I guess those two years were the happiest I ever spent. They were growing years for me. From a spindly kid, I grew into a man. I wore my hair the way the Indians did, in two braids lying across my chest. I learned to ride the way they did, clinging like a burr to the horse's back. I got so I could disappear on either side of the horse, leaving only part of an arm and one foot visible from the other side. Nobody can hit anything with a rifle from a running horse, but we'd fire from beneath our horse's necks and yell like crazy men. It was supposed to scare our enemies.

I was allowed to wear a single eagle feather in my hair for a coup I had counted against a Pawnee while Bent and I and some other Cheyenne braves were on a horse stealing raid. I hadn't killed the Pawnee but had only galloped close to him and touched him with a coup stick. The Cheyenne thinks this takes more courage than killing an enemy, and I suppose they're right. I know I was pretty damn scared while I was doing it.

It was a good life and well suited to a young buck's temperament. There was a lot of hunting because Indians live by hunting buffalo. I learned things I guess nobody could learn that hadn't lived with the Indians. I learned, for instance, how to capture eagles for their feathers. You dig a pit and roof it with branches and brush and bait it with a live rabbit or a live young deer tied to the branches. The eagle comes down and grabs the bait and you reach up through the branches and grab him by the leg.

When you do that, you've got trouble, believe you me. That eagle tears at you with his beak, he claws you with his talons and he half beats you to death with his wings. While he's doing this, you're holding on with one hand and trying to kill him with the knife you've got in the other one.

I learned a lot of other things as well. I learned to make arrows and arrowheads and how to tell from looking at an arrow which tribe had made it, maybe even which arrowmaker. I learned about the secret societies the Indians have, which aren't too much different from those that white men have. Most important of all, I learned to read the ground like white men read their books. I learned to read trails that most white men can't even see. All this time I almost forgot there was a world of white men to which I properly belonged.

I got a crush on a girl named Little Deer and I mooned over her like any lovesick buck. I waited hours sometimes beside the path she'd use going to fetch water for her ma. I played at night on a lute Charles helped me make in front of her pa's lodge until he'd throw something out the flap and yell at me.

All too quickly the second summer passed, and winter came, and now there was trouble between the white men and the Indians. The young braves went out raiding ranches and stagecoaches and wagon trains. They stole horses and sometimes they killed the white men's cows just for the sport of it.

But a lot of things were blamed on the Indians that were done by whites against other whites. And there were white men who sold whisky to the Indians, and guns and powder and lead, and from these things trouble always came.

Storms blew in from the north and the grass was covered and our village camped on Sand Creek along with another, larger village whose chief was Black Kettle and with six or eight lodges of Arapahoe, who were friends of the Cheyenne. Farther east was a larger camp on a river known as the Smoky Hill.

Both villages had gone in to Fort Lyon to be fed through the winter the way the Indian Agents had told them to. The only trouble was, there wasn't anything to feed them with. So the Agent told them to go on out and hunt and feed themselves. He said no troops would bother them. He said they were under the protection of the government.

The Agent lied or at least he sure was wrong. One cold morning in late fall of 1864, cannon boomed out from the ridge behind the sleeping village. Grapeshot rattled against the hide tipi coverings. Musket balls tore through the air and howling, bearded soldiers charged down the slope, killing everything that moved. . . .

At the crest of the ridge where Benteen elected to halt and dig in, I was helped from my horse. I tried to stand, but I slumped to the ground in spite of everything I could do. I dozed for a while, awaking when the surgeon bent over me, having discovered the bullet wound in my side.

He cleaned and bandaged the wound and gave me morphine for the pain. A sergeant gave me a long drink of whisky from a canteen of the stuff that he'd managed to hide someplace in his gear. Lieutenant Payne stuck a cigar in my mouth and lighted it for me.

I heard Benteen send Lieutenant Hare to hurry the supply train along. He said to bring back a couple of ammunition mules at once. Whatever had drawn the Sioux downstream would not keep them there. They would come back and we would need plenty of ammunition when they did.

I rested, knowing I was going to need all the strength I could muster before this was over with. The popping of guns sounded faintly downstream in the direction of that monstrous Indian camp. Custer must have attacked the villages, I thought. He'd been heading straight for them when I'd seen him last.

It was about four-thirty but it seemed as if it had been a month since we spotted the Sioux pony herd from the Crow's Nest at dawn today. The sergeant brought me his canteen of whisky again and I took another drink. Not long afterward I began to feel better and sat up to look around.

The shooting downstream was plainer now, maybe because the wind had changed. It sounded like a Fourth of July celebration, with the distant guns making noises like firecrackers going off in strings. I wished I could see his face when he finally realized how many Indians had surrounded him, when he finally realized he was going to die.

I struggled to my feet with difficulty. I could walk fairly well using my rifle as a cane to steady myself and to keep from falling down. Captain Weir of D Troop was standing by himself staring to the north, grumbling that Reno ought to go to Custer's support immediately.

My head was reeling as I walked toward Weir. Lieutenant Edgerly approached him ahead of me. Weir said, "Damn it, Edgerly, I'm going to get permission from the major to go help General Custer out. Will you go with me if I do?"

Edgerly nodded. Weir stamped away to look for Reno and get permission from him to leave. I stared at Edgerly. Reno wouldn't give permission for Troop D to leave, I thought. He'd be stupid if he did.

A few minutes later I saw Captain Weir ride out toward the north alone. Immediately Lieutenant Edgerly yelled to the men of D Troop to mount and follow him. Those remaining wearily mounted their horses and straggled out toward the north, toward a useless death, I thought. Of what use to Custer would this single company be? Of what effect against the thousands of Sioux separating it and Custer's besieged command?

Edgerly turned and looked at me. I knew he wanted me to come along. I told myself I was a fool for doing it but I found my horse, mounted and, with my head reeling both from whisky and morphine, hurried after him.

Custer's six hundred were scattered to hell and gone, and now Weir was scattering the command even more. Custer was north of us in the direction of the Indian camp. Mathey and McDougall, with the pack train, were back in the direction from which we had come earlier. There must have been at least a dozen men left in the grove when we rode out. The officers of the 7th should be assembling the command, not further dispersing it.

I urged my horse to greater speed and at last caught up with Weir. I said, "Captain, splitting the command isn't going to help anyone. Custer is beyond your help. You couldn't get to him with ten times this many men."

Weir stared at me, coldness in his eyes. "You'd like us to abandon him, wouldn't you?"

I asked, "What are you talking about?"

"I'm talking about you. You were the one General Hazen sent to bring in the Cheyenne back in '68, weren't you? You were living with the Cheyenne, weren't you? And when Custer jumped them on the Washita, that messed up everything for you."

I guess I must have looked surprised because

he said, "You didn't think anyone knew, did you, Lorette?"

I shook my head. "No, I didn't. How did you find out?"

"Never mind. It isn't important anyway. But don't think I'm going to take your advice not to try and reach the general."

I shrugged. I could feel the warmth of blood soaking the arm bandage and also soaking the one around my ribs. I was a fool. I should have stayed with Reno on the knoll. It was now doubtful if either Weir or Edgerly would listen to anything I said.

The exhausted troop toiled along, moving steadily deeper into the barren hills. Suddenly I thought again of Major Elliot, whom Custer had abandoned at the Washita.

Custer must now feel the way Elliot had felt. He must be wondering where the rest of his command was, why they did not come to support him when he so desperately needed them.

Thinking of Elliot and the Washita got me to thinking about the things that had led to my part in that murderous episode. Perhaps weakness had much to do with my wandering thoughts. But as we rode through the shallow hills, my mind once more began wandering in the past.

Little Deer, the Cheyenne girl I'd had the crush on, died at Sand Creek that November morning so long ago and so did her father. Charles Bent was taken prisoner. His brother George and I were both wounded but we managed to escape.

All day we dragged ourselves along through the snow, leading a small party of survivors east toward the camp on the Smoky Hill. George had a bullet in his hip and hobbled along with the aid of a crutch made from a branch. He never complained or mentioned pain. I had a bullet in my shoulder and I'd lost a lot of blood. I was pretty weak.

I wouldn't have believed white men capable of such cruelty if I hadn't seen it with my own eyes in the Cheyenne village on Sand Creek. Men and women both had been mutilated by the knives of the vengeful volunteers. Babies and children had been killed deliberately. I had seen one woman with her belly ripped open by a knife, her bloody, unborn child lying beside her in the snow. In that hour I turned my back on my white heritage. I became wholly Indian.

I fled south with the Indians and for the next

three years I stayed with them. I participated in raids against the whites and because of coups I counted, I was eventually entitled to wear six eagle feathers in my hair.

In September of 1868, General Hazen was sent to Fort Cobb on the Washita by General Sherman to implement the Medicine Lodge Treaty by persuading the Cheyenne and Kiowa to settle on their reservations south of the Kansas line. He sent out a runner to look for me.

Not quite knowing whether I was going to be killed or not, I went in to Fort Cobb and talked with him. He wanted me to take on the job of bringing the Indians in. I spoke the Cheyenne tongue like one of the Cheyenne, he said. I was trusted by the Indians because I had been wounded and bereaved at Sand Creek. If there was a man alive who could bring the Indians in, he said, I was that man.

I took the job, but only because I knew what the consequences would be to the Indians if they did not come in. I went out, alone, and traveled several hundred miles in a few weeks time. Among the chiefs I persuaded to settle on the reservation was Black Kettle, whose village was the one Chivington had attacked at Sand Creek four years earlier. I gave Black Kettle General Hazen's guarantee that he would be safe if he came in. I also gave him my personal guarantee. Having seen all the Cheyenne chiefs within two hundred miles, I returned to Fort Cobb to report.

I can still remember waking on that November morning following my return to hear a Cheyenne runner babbling excitedly about the attack. I can still remember the biting cold, and the snow, as I set out for Black Kettle's village with half a dozen Agency Indian scouts.

For twenty-four hours we pushed our horses northwest along the course of the Washita. The stripped and mutilated bodies of Elliot and his men were the first ones that we reached.

Buzzards circled above the dead. Wolves prowled, turning and showing their snarling teeth but staying out of range.

I got down from my horse and walked among the bodies of Elliot and his men. The Cheyenne had stripped them of their uniforms but a bit of bright metal caught my eye. I picked it up and saw that it was the insignia of the 7th Cavalry.

I mounted again and led the Agency Indians a couple of miles farther on until we came to the gutted, still-smoldering village of Black Kettle.

Here the dead lay scattered like broken dolls. Here, the snow was tramped by the shod hoofs of hundreds of cavalry mounts. Here the story of the dawn attack could be plainly read in the trampled snow.

Going on, I saw the eight hundred Indian horses that had been shot by Custer and his men. Some still lived in the midst of that awesome pile of slaughtered flesh. Wolves prowled among the carcasses, too gorged to eat but snarling and fighting among themselves.

I was physically sick at the sights and sounds. I was sick at heart because I knew that part of the responsibility for what had happened here was mine. I had persuaded Black Kettle to bring his village in. I had added my own guarantee of safety to that of the general.

Up on the ridge a file of mounted Cheyenne warriors suddenly appeared. Their feathers fluttered in the wind. The manes and tails of their horses bannered out. Their leader raised his rifle above his head and his horse leaped toward me down the slope.

Their shrill cries ripped through the biting air. And suddenly I knew that I was a Cheyenne no more. I had betrayed them, or so they thought.

They weren't going to give me an opportunity to explain.

I glanced around at the Agency Indian scouts. In their faces I saw shock, cold fury, hate. I wheeled my horse and dug my heels into his trembling sides.

Back down the valley I ran the horse, with the Cheyenne and the Agency Indians in hot pursuit. I got away and managed to reach Fort Cobb, but I knew that from that day on I would be an alien to the Cheyenne, an enemy. They would kill me on sight. This, then, was the reason I had hated the general. Custer had led the 7th to the Washita.

X

EDGERLY PULLED a watch from his pocket, opened the hunting case and glanced at it. He turned, saw the question in my eyes and said wearily, "It's almost five o'clock. God, it seems like ten hours since the general told Major Reno to charge the Sioux. It has actually been less than three."

Ahead, Weir had pulled his horse to a sudden halt. Edgerly rode up beside him and I halted beside Edgerly.

From this high ridge we could see the valley of the Little Big Horn for almost a dozen miles. We could see the entire Sioux encampment at last.

It was impossible to count the lodges. A man could only estimate. But there were thousands of them, strung along the stream bank for at least a mile.

Farther from the stream, between the village and the bluffs, was the shifting pony herd we had glimpsed through the dust from the Crow's Nest this morning, the pony herd in whose existence Custer had so stubbornly refused to believe. And on a hill, three miles away, mounted Indians swarmed like ants whose anthill has been stirred up with a stick. Custer and his five troops were nowhere to be seen.

Weir raised an arm and signaled for Troop D to go on. He started his horse down into the next ravine. I called. "Captain, think! You don't even know where Custer is. There must be at least three thousand Indians down there and you have less than forty men. You can think what you like of me but at least wait until Mathey and McDougall arrive with the pack train escort."

Weir glanced coldly at me and I knew he was probably going to ignore my advice. He said, "Go back and tell them where we have gone. Bring them along after us if they'll come."

I looked after him, wondering why the United States Army had to have so many goddam fools in it. Then I turned my horse and headed back toward Reno and Benteen and what remained of their two commands.

No sooner was I out of sight of D Troop than a half dozen skulking Sioux galloped toward me out of nowhere, screeching like maniacs. Only one of them had a gun, an ancient flintlock. The others had bows and arrows, knives and tomahawks. I whacked my horse's rump with my carbine barrel and he lunged up a steep, dusty slope only half a dozen yards ahead of the Indians.

The main body of Sioux may have ridden north but there were still plenty of skulking Sioux around looking for a chance to count an easy coup. And if Custer was, as I believed, under attack near the villages, the braves attacking him would be coming back here as soon as they had defeated him.

My head felt light and my senses reeled from

the horse's rough gait plunging up that slope. Behind me, the Indians were yelling still. One threw his tomahawk, a steel-headed one, and it missed my head by less than a foot. I heard the unmistakable sound of an arrow leaving a bow. The arrow went by so close I could feel its wind and the whistling sound it made.

I turned in my saddle, aimed hastily, and fired. One of the bucks was driven backward out of his saddle. I aimed again.

The others pulled up, their faces surprised. They were all very young, without battle experience. I reached the top of the ridge and sent my horse leaping down into the next ravine. By the time the bucks pursuing me reached the ridge top behind me, I was already climbing out of the ravine toward the ridge beyond.

At the crest of it, I caught a glimpse of blue-clad troopers ahead of me. I saw Lieutenant Hare coming in with two ammunition mules. They were pulling back stubbornly against their halter ropes. A trooper behind them repeatedly lashed them with a length of rope.

Movement behind the two mules drew my glance. The rest of the pack train was straggling up the long slope, harried on two sides and in the rear by forty or fifty galloping Indians. Troopers rode on both sides of the lumbering mules, holding the Indians off, firing with such accuracy that the Indians drew back, screeching, out of range.

Things were looking better all the time. Benteen's three troops had joined Reno's battered command. Now the mule train and the troopers escorting it had reached the six companies. Our depleted ammunition supply would be replenished and we would have food and medical supplies. With luck and with no more foolishness like chasing off to try and find Custer, there was a bare chance we would be able to hold out until Crook or Terry and Gibbon could arrive.

I rode to Reno immediately. "Major, Captain Weir and Lieutenant Edgerly sent me back to request that you bring the command along after them."

Reno looked surprised. "Where the hell have those two gone?"

Apparently, then, Weir had not obtained permission to take D Troop and go to Custer's assistance. I said, "Captain Weir rode out alone, Major, to see if he could locate Custer and his men. The lieutenant likely thought you had given permission for D Troop to go, because he took the troop and followed. The captain sent me back . . ."

"All right. All right. I heard you, Lorette."

Benteen approached. His face was calm, if a little redder than usual. There was none of Reno's harried nervousness in him. He said, "What's going on, Lorette?"

"Captain Weir and Lieutenant Edgerly have gone into the hills north of here to look for General Custer, Captain Benteen. They sent me back to bring the rest of the command along."

I was facing toward the river as I talked. Suddenly I saw men approaching at a gallop up the slope. I saw a figure in buckskins riding at their head. It was Herendeen. Behind him rode eleven troopers, who had, apparently, been abandoned in the grove of trees on the riverbank earlier when Reno pulled out so precipitously.

Benteen turned his head and stared at them. He walked away suddenly, and approached Herendeen. "Are there any more down there?"

"Only the dead, Captain."

Beside me, Reno shouted. "Herendeen!"

"Yes sir." Herendeen approached.

"Why didn't you and these troopers withdraw from that grove with the rest of the command?"

"We didn't hear the order, Major. Wasn't no

trumpet call. And there was some noise down there, a heap of noise."

"All right." Reno seemed to hesitate. At last he said, "We'll move out in the direction D Troop has gone. Issue ammunition to all the men. Make litters for the wounded. We will try to find General Custer if we can."

I stared around at the exhausted command. There were now close to three hundred here, half of the original six hundred with which Custer had entered the valley at dawn. They had marched all day yesterday and most of the night. They had marched all day today and had been under fire for more than two hours. There was not much left in them, I thought. They couldn't stand much more. But they had to stand it because they had no other choice. God only knew where Terry and Gibbon were. God only knew where Crook was with his thousand men.

Men began trying to make litters to carry the wounded on. There was no timber for carrying poles, so wounded men were placed on blankets, with a trooper carrying at each of the four corners. Horse holders were to bring the horses along. Troopers with the mule train were trying to repack some of those whose packs were slipping or likely to come undone.

It suddenly came to me that this was Sunday. Back at Fort Abraham Lincoln the chaplain was planning evening services. In Dodge City, people were dressing to go to church. It seemed impossible.

I saw Lieutenant Payne and walked to him, leading my horse. My head was reeling and I thought I was going to fall down. I sat down on the rump of a dead horse and let my head hang between my knees. Payne said, "Miles, is there anything I can do for you?"

I shook my head. He knelt in front of me. "Want a cigar?"

I nodded and he handed one to me. I stuck it in my mouth and he struck a match and held it for me. I took several puffs on the cigar. My head began to clear.

Payne said, "I thought I'd be glad when Custer got what was coming to him but I'm not. All I can think of is the two hundred and twenty-five men he had with him."

"You don't know that Custer's dead."

"The firing has stopped, Miles. The firing has stopped down there toward the villages."

"Maybe he drove them off."

Payne shook his head. "I don't think so, Miles. I don't think so." There was shock in his eyes. He believed that half the 7th Cavalry was gone, that Custer's invincible command had been defeated by the Indians he had said he could get through in a single day. And he knew it wasn't over yet.

XI

THREE HUNDRED men, many wounded seriously. A hundred and sixty mules, worn out and balky, inexpertly packed. Nearly three hundred cavalry mounts in charge of horse holders, four horses to a man. The 7th Cavalry was beaten but had not yet admitted it. What remained of it would now move out to render assistance to Custer and his five companies.

Reno and Benteen led off, with Benteen's H Troop. Godfrey's K came next. Behind K Troop came the horse holders and the worn horses, heads hanging, moving placidly, and behind the horses came the mules, some of their packs sagging to right or left, ropes and girths dangling. Behind the mules came the wounded, carried on blankets by four troopers each. One man screamed with the pain of being lifted and immediately lost consciousness. Others moaned intermittently. One laid back, grinning, smoking a cigar and blowing smoke insolently at his bearers, ignoring the shredded, bleeding flesh of his right leg. Reno's three battered troops brought up the rear.

A corporal, whose name I didn't know, and three others, offered to carry me on a blanket but I refused. I was still able to ride and the motion of my horse would be no more painful than the motion of the crude litter they offered me.

I accepted help in mounting, however, and clung to the saddle as my horse moved out with the column, heading north toward the Sioux villages. I knew we ought to stay on this high knoll and spend our energy digging in. As soon as the Sioux were through with Custer and his five companies they would be coming after us. They might already be on the way. Payne had said the firing had stopped in the direction Custer had gone earlier. But I wasn't in command. Reno was and he had let the veiled criticism of his junior officers color his judgment. He knew better than to go charging off to attack the Sioux but he was going anyway.

I found myself traveling with Captain Moylan's A Troop, which had suffered heavily in the grove of trees down on the valley floor before Benteen arrived. The men looked haggard, spent. A number of them had superficial wounds which had not been dressed. All had beard stubble on their faces. All were grimed with dust. All had red-rimmed eyes and chapped, cracked lips.

I heard one private growl, "Why the hell do we have to go help Custer out? He didn't come and support us like he said he would."

Another man said, "Shut up, Broyles. There are five troops with the general. That's who we're goin' to help."

The head of the column dropped into the first ravine and climbed out again. The rest of the men staggered along, blindly following. A few Indians watched from a ridge a quarter mile away.

Dust still boiled up in the direction we were traveling, raised by the gigantic horse herd and by the mounted Sioux galloping back and forth. At the crest of each successive ridge, I would catch a glimpse of the village and of the valley beyond.

We were like men walking to the scaffold, to our own execution, I thought sourly. Custer was surely gone by now and so were his five companies. Reno would throw this command to destruction in a vain attempt to save those who were already lost.

As numb with pain and exhaustion as the men around me, I let my head sag forward, let the horse pick his own way along. I closed my eyes and for a little while I dozed.

My dreams were vivid for all that I was only half asleep. I was riding again with the Cheyenne, hunting buffalo, stealing horses from the Pawnees. I was waking in the village on Sand Creek that November morning and hearing the guns and the savage yells of Chivington's hundred-day volunteers.

A hand on my arm wakened me and I discovered Lieutenant Payne striding along close to me. "You fell asleep, Miles. You were about to fall out of your saddle."

I nodded. Ahead I could now see the troops of Weir and Edgerly on their hilltop promontory. Halted, they were waiting for Reno and the main body of the command to arrive. They were still half a mile away.

Reno's command was strung out for a quarter mile. The head of it was down in a ravine, its rear guard in another ravine two ridges back. Glancing around, I saw that more Indians were now watching us, plainly visible against the skyline half a mile away.

The men with the mules flayed them viciously, cursing with frustrated rage. A horse will travel until he drops but a mule will not. The mules wanted to stop. Only the savage beating kept them moving on.

I wondered where General Crook was with his thousand men. I wondered where Gibbon and Terry were. They were supposed to arrive in the valley of the Little Big Horn on June 26. That had been the battle plan. It was ironic that Custer, by attacking a day too soon, had cheated himself of Terry's support and of the victory he wanted so desperately.

My head felt light, as though I was slightly drunk. I hadn't had but two drinks of whisky, so it couldn't be only that. It was probably a combination of weakness from my wounds and the effects of the morphine the surgeon had given me. But the pain didn't bother me as much as it had previously and I knew the morphine was having its effect.

Moylan and Payne and I dropped down into the last ravine and began to climb out on the other side. Firing suddenly crackled spasmodically ahead. Moylan and Payne ran up the last steep slope and I heeled my horse after them. I rode out on the top of the last promontory where D Troop had remained.

Weir and Edgerly had dismounted their men. Horse holders had retreated behind the top of the promontory to protect the horses from being hit. The men of D Troop fired steadily from kneeling and prone positions at the Sioux now charging up the slope. H Troop and K had deployed to right and left and were also firing.

I stared at the approaching Indians. From this elevation it was possible to see the full and awesome extent of the Sioux force riding toward us.

In front rode those with the fastest mounts, scattered, reckless, darting in the slash and withdraw the way wolves attack a buffalo they know is still dangerous. But behind these reckless few . . . behind these few the plain was hidden by Sioux warriors trotting their horses unhurriedly.

Their earlier excitement seemed to be almost completely gone. A flash of cavalry blue caught my eye and I saw one buck wearing a cavalry sergeant's coat, its chevrons flaming yellow against the background of dusty blue. Another was wearing a campaign hat over his braids. Others brandished cavalry Springfields, trophies . . .

Perhaps they had taken these things from Reno's men, killed escaping from the grove of trees along the river earlier. He had lost nearly half his command before Benteen arrived. Or perhaps they had been taken from Custer's men . . .

There wasn't time to speculate. The solid wall of trotting Indians now kicked and whipped their ponies into a run. Shrill cries broke from their lips. Ten feet away from me Moylan bawled, "Deploy to the left! Move, goddam it, move!"

The men of A Troop, scurried left, taking a hasty position on the command's left flank. The wall of Indians charged up the slope . . .

A blue cloud of powdersmoke lifted on the light breeze from the cavalry firing line. Once more I heard that strange kind of roar, a sound compounded of many sounds, the drum of horses' hoofs against the ground, the booming roar of the cavalry carbines, the crack of officers' revolvers, the shouts and cries of men, the shrill, yipping cries of the attacking Indians, the nickering of terrified horses and the bray of balky mules.

I slid from my horse's back. I made too damn good a target sitting there. I released the reins and the horse trotted toward the other horses on the back side of the knoll, head turned to one side so he would not step on the trailing reins.

This position was a precarious one. Hills rose behind it, hills that would be occupied by Sioux sharpshooters as soon as the attack wave broke around us. Mule train and horses were being held in the ravine immediately behind this little knoll, and would also be exposed to fire from higher knolls and ridges to the east.

I knelt beside Lieutenant Payne and checked the loads in my Spencer carbine. I began firing.

A Troop's marksmanship was terrible. Excited and desperate, the men fired straight into the attacking wave, not bothering to pick out individual targets, trusting to luck, I suppose, that they would hit something.

I knew the quickest way to discourage attacking Indians was to inflict heavy losses on them. I picked each target carefully and with each shot knocked a galloping Indian off of his horse. Beside me, Payne was doing as well, steadying his revolver with his left hand while he fired it with his right.

On my left a trooper suddenly leaped to his feet. An arrow projected from his chest. With both hands, he frantically tried to pull it out. He staggered down the hill toward the attacking Indians, oblivious of them, oblivious of everything but his anxiety to get the arrow out.

The shaft broke in his hands and he stood there swaying, looking down at it as though he could not understand its breaking off. Then he fell face down on the slope and afterward laid still.

The wave of Indians broke around us like water breaking around a rock in the middle of a stream. They had nearly surrounded us. They were already on the high ground to our rear, firing down with a demoralizing effect on the horse holders and the men with the balky mules.

I turned my head and looked at Payne. "We'd better get the hell out of here, Lieutenant, or we won't get out at all."

He turned his head and yelled at Moylan, "Captain, they're surrounding us!"

Moylan nodded. He turned and stared toward Reno and Benteen. I studied the troopers' faces on both sides of me. They were grimly determined but they were also mighty scared.

Reno spoke to Benteen, who got to his feet and

roared, "Fall back! D Troop and A will form a rear guard!"

Horse holders began to retreat with the troopers' mounts. The mules were whipped into motion once again. Reno led Benteen's H Troop down the slope into the ravine and beyond to try and drive a wedge into the thin scattering of Sioux at the column's rear. He led a charge up the far side of the ravine, splitting the mounted warriors to right and left, making an opening through which the command could retreat toward the position it had held earlier.

My carbine barrel was smoking. I reloaded it. I'd been in plenty of tight spots but always before there had seemed to be a way out. I was damned if I could see a way out of this. The slope below us was littered with the bodies of Indians we had either wounded or killed, but more kept coming all the time. And behind those fighting us were hundreds, thousands, who had not yet been able to get close enough to get in their licks at us.

The Sioux began to yell more shrilly, more triumphantly when they saw we were beginning to withdraw. And even more recklessly they rode in to the attack.

XII

THE PRESSURE on Weir's D Troop and on the ragged remnant of A was terrible. Weir stood his ground with his men, erect, exposing himself deliberately to give steadiness and confidence to his men. He was feeling now, for the first time, I thought, the terrible pressure that had been applied to Reno's three troops earlier down on the valley floor.

I glanced out into the boiling dust cloud and over the heads of the attacking Indians, looking for some sign of Custer and his men. If they were out there they were dead, I thought. The only hope that they might still be alive lay in the possibility that they had retreated deeper into the hills lying east of the valley of the Little Horn.

But there wasn't time to worry about Custer and his five troops. There was only time to fight. An Indian buck, a young and reckless one, rode his horse in close, leaning down to take a swipe at me with a steel-headed tomahawk. I reversed my gun and drove the butt squarely into his face. The tomahawk grazed the muscles of my back, ripping through shirt and underwear, bringing blood instantly. From the way it felt, I knew it wasn't a deep wound. It was only a grazing one, painful but not serious.

The Indian's horse carried him beyond me, unconscious or already dead. He fell from the horse's back, rolled limply for a couple of yards, and then lay still. A trooper near him smashed his skull with his carbine butt before returning his attention to others galloping in behind.

Wave after wave came in, on fresh horses, eager for the kill. I heard a man bawl, "Sarge, I'm out of ammunition!"

The sergeant's voice roared back, "Then take a couple of men and go get some more! Move, damn it! The rest of us are going to run out pretty soon!"

Captain Moylan yelled, "Make every shot count! Make every bullet bring one of those red devils down!"

Glancing around, I saw there was open space between us and the nearest of the other, retreating troops. Weir and Moylan must have seen it at almost the same time because they shouted the order to pull back.

A step at a time, we began our slow retreat. The Sioux, inflamed by what seemed to be victory, charged in more recklessly than before. A solid line of them came galloping up the slope, neither slowing nor turning aside before the deadly volley of rifle fire that ripped into them. Riderless horses veered away, but the rest came on. Their horses bowled some of the troopers off their feet. The line of Indians went through us, and past us, then turned to come charging back.

Empty rifles clubbed, the dusty-faced troopers fought grimly, desperately. For a few minutes we were an island, surrounded, pounded mercilessly from all sides. Captain Weir, his hat gone, blood smeared over one side of his face, led a charge that made contact with the retreating column, and after that we kept closed up, maintaining a tighter formation to prevent a repetition of what had just occurred.

Payne fought beside me, retreating a few steps at a time. I glanced at him. His eyes were narrowed but very bright and intent. He squeezed off each shot carefully, deliberately. When he paused to reload his revolver; he turned his head and looked at me. His eyes were immediately concerned. I suppose I looked pretty weak. I felt weak but I had no intention of giving into weakness now. If a man fell here he'd be hacked to pieces before anyone could get to him.

I glanced around. We were backing out of the ravine, with a momentary advantage because we were higher than the Sioux attacking us. Down in the bottom of the ravine, among the milling horde of Indian bucks, I caught a glimpse of a light-colored campaign hat that I instantly recognized. It had belonged to Captain Keogh, the wild Irishman, the soldier of fortune who had once been a Papal zouave.

I reached out and touched Lieutenant Payne's arm. I pointed at the Indian wearing the hat.

Payne glanced at him, then back at me. His teeth were white as he yelled, "Keogh could have lost his hat! Reno lost his and so did Weir!"

I nodded but was not convinced. I was thinking of the way the Indians had deliberately withdrawn from their earlier attack on us. Only something of greater importance could have made them pull away like that.

Afterward, we had heard distant firing down the valley in the direction of the Indian villages. And when the firing stopped, the Sioux had returned and attacked us again. In my mind, it added up to just one thing. Custer had met the Sioux and a fierce battle had been fought, ending in the annihilation of the general and his five companies. The parts of uniforms we saw now on the Sioux attacking us had come from Custer's men as well as from Reno's dead in the river grove.

Not that it mattered particularly. Custer couldn't get to us, even if he was still alive. Nor could we get to him. We had tried and failed. The best we could hope for would be to reach the same high promontory to which Reno and Benteen had earlier withdrawn. There we might stand a chance of surviving until Terry and Gibbon could arrive. Not a very good chance but a chance.

Beside me a trooper fell, an arrow in his thigh. He was up immediately, limping along, using his carbine as a crutch. Another trooper went down with a bullet in his chest. I stopped and stood over him, firing steadily, while two other troopers got him between them and carried him toward the rear.

We reached the crest of the second ridge. Over the racket of battle, the gunshots, the yells, the pound of horses' hoofs, I heard Captain Weir yelling something but I could not make out what it was. I understood quickly, though, when I saw the bulk of the rear guard continue down into the next ravine, helping the wounded or carrying them. A handful of men stayed on the crest of the ridge, kneeling, firing with fatalistic steadiness. Weir had kept his veterans on the ridge, men who had fought before, both in the war and at the Washita.

Payne stayed on the ridge and I did too. The morphine the surgeon had given me must have been wearing off because I was in more pain than before. My left arm, the one with the arrow wound, was so stiff I could hardly use it to steady my rifle. I could feel the warmth of blood soaking the bandage over it. I could also feel blood soaking the bandage around my ribs.

Glancing around, I saw the last of the main column go over the ridge behind us. The retreating rear guard was halfway up the slope. Weir yelled an order and the line of veterans got up and backed slowly down the slope.

Howling, the Sioux attacked from the crest of the ridge we had just left. Our line wavered and gave before the pressure of that charge. I was knocked rolling when a Sioux horse struck me head-on. I narrowly missed being trampled beneath his hoofs. I held onto my rifle, though, knowing if I lost it I was finished. I struggled to my hands and knees.

Indians seemed to be all around us. Only the fact that they were mounted and that we were afoot kept us from being wiped out instantly. Those of us who were left formed a hollow square. I told myself that now we were going to die.

Suddenly I saw a face among the Indians that I knew. It was that of a Cheyenne called Yellow Foot. He recognized me at the same instant and charged straight toward me.

I raised my rifle and sighted carefully. I saw him driven aside out of his saddle. He disappeared into the melee of horseflesh and screaming Indians.

Payne was still on his feet and so was Weir. I heard a trumpeter blowing the charge from the ridge behind us. The bugle's notes were clear and unbelievably sweet because they promised life when death had been a certainty. I glanced around fleetingly, long enough to see a line of mounted troopers charging down the long slope toward us.

Godfrey rode in front, waving his revolver in

the air. The line undulated as Reno's charging line had earlier today, then straightened and came on. It reached the bottom of the ravine. The troopers leaped their horses across and came charging up the slope.

Weir roared something that I didn't catch because of all the other noise. The hollow square broke as the line of charging cavalrymen passed and we ran unashamedly to the bottom of the ravine and on up the slope beyond.

It was littered with discarded equipment, with articles fallen from the backs of the mules. There were three dead horses here and a dead mule, his pack still on his back. A dead trooper lay beside the mule. A couple of men tried to drag the trooper up the slope with them but gave up when they began to fall dangerously behind.

Godfrey's mounted troop turned and galloped back toward us, about a third of them fighting a rear guard action to cover the retreat. At the ridge top the troop halted, giving the fighting third a chance to rejoin them there.

The knoll we had evacuated earlier was now visible toward the south. The head of Reno's column had reached it. Even at this distance I could see the way the troopers spread to its sides to form an immediate defense.

The commander of the 7th Cavalry had been a glory-hunting fool. He had led his men into a situation from which there might well be no escape. But he would have been proud of these men if he could have seen them now. There were no slackers, no cowards in their midst. Grimly, efficiently, each man did what must be done.

Godfrey's K Troop dismounted. Horse holders galloped their horses toward us, and passed us, and went on to rejoin the main body of the command. Dismounted, K Troop fought a fierce rear guard action, retreating a few steps at a time. They dropped into the ravine, backed up the slope and across the ridge and down into the next ravine, contesting every foot of the way.

Their failure to overwhelm us seemed to infuriate the Sioux. Their shrieks rose to a higher pitch. I could see the glowing ball of the sun shining through the overcast. It was low in the western sky and from its position I judged it must be well past six.

My belly felt hollow, reminding me I'd had nothing to eat since morning. Not even a drink of water. Nor would I get anything, at least before darkness fell. There would be no rest, no food, not

even water as long as it was light because while
there was light the Sioux would not let up.

It seemed to go on forever. It seemed to have
been going on forever. This morning's gathering
of scouts and officers at the Crow's Nest seemed
to have been a thousand years ago. Pain was constant, like a branding iron in my shoulder and side
and across my back. My head felt light, sometimes
felt as if it floated above my body. My rifle was
empty and while I reloaded it, I turned my back
on the Indians and trudged up the slope as if I was
all alone. I saw Payne watching me as if he was
waiting for me to fall. I tried to grin at him but it
didn't feel much like a grin.

I was thinking about the Washita again when I
turned and began to fire once more at the Indians.
My eyes began to water and my vision blurred,
but anger had renewed my strength. I doubt if I
hit any Sioux during the remainder of our retreat
to the crest of the knoll but I kept firing.

Noise was constant all the way. It was the noise
of battle, never changing, always the same. But
once we reached the knoll the sounds were different. Here there were moans, of wounded men
in pain. Here there were screams, from the dying,
from those the surgeon tried to help. Here there

was the confusion of men trying to bring order out of chaos, to establish a defense against the indefensible. And all the time the Sioux kept slashing at our perimeter, with uncounted thousands in reserve.

The 7th was cornered and at bay. I sat down on the rump of a dead horse. I suddenly felt the sleep loss of the past few days. I let my head droop forward and closed my eyes. But I couldn't sleep. The past kept parading through my mind.

After the slaughter on the Washita there wasn't much else I could do but return to the way of the whites. That meant I had to get a job. It meant I had to earn my keep.

General Hazen gave me a temporary job, driving a freight wagon between Fort Cobb and Dodge. I threw away my buckskins and got me some white men's clothes. I cut my hair and grew a beard. I sure didn't want to be recognized in case any wandering Cheyenne jumped the wagon train.

I was twenty-two the year following the Washita, and I was pretty dumb. I had never tasted whisky nor fought another man with my fists, nor bedded a woman who had white skin.

That first visit to Dodge, I did all three. I loaded my wagon and drove it into the circle with the others just outside of town, and then I took off for town. I went into the first saloon and ordered a bottle and a glass. I took it over to a table in the corner and poured myself a drink.

The first one made me gag and I was glad I was by myself. The second and third were just the same and I was beginning to think this had been overrated. I had a few more, these going down easier, and I decided it hadn't been overrated after all. I got up and started out of there and someone got in my way and I knocked him halfway across the room. After that things got kind of mixed up but it must have been one hell of a fight because I was in pretty bad shape when I woke up the next morning in jail.

I started yelling and the marshal came and let me out. I got a room at the hotel and took a bath and shaved, being careful because of all the bruises and skinned places on my face.

I felt mighty alone that day. I stared down into the bustling streets wondering if I could learn to live the way these people did, knowing too that I didn't have a choice. The Indians didn't want me any more.

I began hating Custer in earnest, I suppose, that day. And I told myself that before I was through I'd get back at him.

XIII

ANYONE WHO has ever heard a single, crescendo note maintained interminably can imagine the effect of the sustained noise of battle upon the men remaining in Major Reno's command. They were demoralized and near their breaking point. They believed that Custer and all the men of his five companies had been slaughtered, stripped and mutilated. They believed they would share Custer's fate, that it was only a matter of time until they did.

Reno was nearly as demoralized as they. He keenly felt the criticism implied in Weir's attempt to reach the general. He also believed Custer and his men were dead. He believed he and his own command were soon to die. He was over his depth. He had fought in the war against men like himself. He had never fought Indians, had never faced such overwhelming odds.

Benteen took over the defense and Reno permitted it. Stocky, red-faced, no longer benign, Benteen's blue eyes flashed and his shouted orders reached the men for whom they were intended despite the roar of battle noise and the cries of wounded and dying men. "Wallace," he bawled, "form your troop here!"

"Troop?" Wallace asked breathlessly, trying to grin. "Captain, I have only three men!"

"Very good. Form your three men here!"

Wallace obeyed. Benteen shouted, "Godfrey, form K Troop here!"

Godfrey obeyed without question despite the fact that Benteen held the same rank as he. Benteen moved on and gradually out of the melee of men and animals, order began to emerge. There was a hollow in the plateau or knoll to which we had retreated, and to this hollow Benteen directed the men to bring the wounded and the horses and the mules.

I continued to sit wearily on the dead horse. For the moment I didn't care if I got hit by one of the Sioux bullets still tearing into the massed horses and men here on the knoll. I was beat and near exhaustion. Pain was so constant I had trouble making my mind function. Death seemed preferable to a continuance of the pain.

Head hanging, I waited for my weakness to pass. I wasn't thinking or remembering any more. I wasn't thinking of Custer, or the Washita, or of my former Cheyenne friends. My mind was numb.

I heard Benteen shout, "Get the rest of the packs off those mules! Distribute rations and ammunition to the men!"

And a few minutes later, "Sergeant! Hitch up a team of mules and start dragging these carcasses to where they can be used for bulwarks!"

The firing slackened gradually. The painted horsemen ceased their reckless charges against our position on the knoll.

I heard a voice say, "I have a bit of a nip here, Mr. Lorette, that might help the way you feel."

I glanced up. I accepted the canteen from Sergeant O'Malley of K Troop and gulped a couple of swallows of whisky from it. I managed to grin as I raised my hand to wipe my mouth. I remember thinking, "Thank God for a man that will thumb his nose at regulations and put whisky in his canteen."

A trooper drove a team of mules to the horse I was sitting on and started to wrap a chain around his two hind legs. He said, "You'll have to sit someplace else, Mr. Lorette. I got orders to drag these carcasses to where they'll give protection to the men."

I stood up and watched him drag the horse's carcass away. The whisky was warm in my stomach and while the pain of my wounds had not lessened, I felt better because of it.

I could see what Benteen was doing with the command. He was forming a perimeter of defense in a horseshoe shape, with the open end of the horseshoe toward the bluffs in back of us.

Calmly, imperturbably he strode back and forth, closing a gap here, giving a word of encouragement someplace else.

The firing from the Indians, which had slackened temporarily, now began again. They had moved into position on the higher ground to the north and east of us. They had dismounted and now lay prone in a solid line, mostly hidden and presenting difficult targets at which to shoot. They fired a deadly hail of bullets into the besieged command.

Men yelled hoarsely as they were hit. Horses

and mules, struck, went down kicking, making shrill sounds of terror and of pain. Troopers with them shot the wounded ones, then dragged off their carcasses to give protection to the men defending the edges of the plateau.

I looked around, searching for Lieutenant Payne and Captain Moylan and what was left of A Troop. They had formed on the southwest edge of the knoll facing the valley and the twisting river in the middle of it.

I stumbled toward them and collapsed beside Lieutenant Payne. He glanced at me. "Why the hell don't you go back where the wounded are? Nobody expects you to be up here on the firing line. You need rest and sleep."

"I'll sleep when it gets dark."

Payne laid his rifle on the belly of the dead horse behind which we lay. He sighted carefully and fired. I saw an Indian, who had been all but invisible behind a clump of gray-green sagebrush, jump up, then fall, kicking, to the ground. He heaved a couple of spasmodic breaths and then laid still.

I said, "I think Custer knew at the last how Elliot felt at the Washita. Maybe he also knew how the Indians felt when he jumped them the way he did."

Payne turned his head and looked at me. "He knew. But for some reason that isn't much satisfaction to me. I keep thinking of the two hundred and twenty-five men he had with him."

A bullet, fired from behind a clump of brush on the slope in front of us, tore the throat out of a trooper not ten feet away, on the lieutenant's right. Instantly half a dozen men fired at the clump. There was a movement behind it, and then nothing.

Smoke billowed from behind another clump farther down. Payne said, "The bastards are all over that slope, Miles, behind every clump of brush. They're going to cost us a hell of a lot of casualties unless we get them out of there."

"I'll go back and tell Benteen. Twenty men on horseback could clear them out."

Payne nodded. I got up and moved back toward the center of the plateau, looking for Benteen.

The depression in the center of the plateau held the horses and mules, tied to picket lines. Toward the valley end of the depression the wounded lay, more than fifty of them by now. The surgeon, Dr. Porter, was working as fast as he could, assisted by the medical orderly and half a dozen other men. A fire had been started and over it a kettle boiled, filled with the surgeon's instruments. The water in the kettle was red with blood. Men moaned and cried out. One cursed savagely, continuously. An occasional bullet kicked up a spurt of dust.

I found Captain Benteen on the far side of the horseshoe. I said, "Captain, Lieutenant Payne sent me to tell you there are skulkers behind every clump of sagebrush on the slope in front of him. He thought a mounted charge around the three sides of this knoll might clear them out."

He nodded. He turned his head and roared, "Godfrey! Mount fifteen men! I want you to lead a charge and clear out skulkers on the slope!"

Godfrey got to his feet fifty feet away. He began to shout names and the men whose names he called gathered silently.

I knew most of them. They were the best in Godfrey's troop, the steadiest, the most experienced. They went to the picket line, got their horses and mounted them.

Benteen shouted, "Hold your fire! Hold your fire!" The command was repeated by officers and noncoms down along the line of defenders until it had made the full circle and returned to its starting point.

Benteen nodded at Godfrey, who now swung to the back of his horse. He led his men out, leaving the knoll at the rear, circling left along its slope.

I walked across the knoll to a point from which I could see its slope. Godfrey's fifteen men had formed a galloping line reaching from the bottom of the knoll almost to its top. They were about ten feet apart.

Ahead of them, concealed Indians leaped to their feet from behind their clumps of brush and tried to get away. Some were shot. Some were clubbed by rifle butts. One was knocked down and trampled by a horse.

The line swept around the knoll. One man stood up in his stirrups clutching his belly with both hands. His horse, without control, wheeled and galloped off the slope. He had gone less than a quarter mile before he was enveloped by Indians. The trooper, riddled, fell from his saddle and was briefly dragged along the ground.

The remainder of Godfrey's men returned to the top of the hill. Benteen yelled, "Fire at will," and this command was also repeated down along the line.

I returned to where Payne and Moylan were. It didn't seem strange to me that I should fail to be concerned about the bullets flying around. After being exposed so long a man stops worrying about being hit.

Payne said, "If Custer's really gone, it seems damned strange that he would go this way. After going through the war with only one slight wound."

I asked, "How the hell did he ever get to be a general anyway? He was the youngest general in the Army, wasn't he?"

Payne nodded. "He was brigadier general when he was twenty-three."

"Why? What had he done to deserve it?"

"That's the puzzling part of it. He'd done nothing particularly outstanding. But he *had* caught General McClellan's eye. He was either promoted at McClellan's insistence or it was a mistake. Anyway, when he made general they gave him the Michigan Brigade."

"And I'll bet the Michigan liked him no better than the 7th does."

Payne grinned. "No better. For a man who had been the sloppiest, most insubordinate cadet in his class at West Point, he was one hell of a tough disciplinarian with the troops under him. They hated him. But he made soldiers out of them. I'll say that much for him."

He stared out across the dusty valley. Indians and horses still milled around out there, uncounted thousands of them. Almost as though he was talking to himself, Payne said, "I wonder if we're going to get out of this."

I glanced at his face. It was sombre and for a moment filled with regret. I asked, "Thinking about your family?"

He nodded. "My boy is fifteen. He wants to go to West Point when he's old enough. My daughter is thirteen."

"Where are they? At Fort Lincoln?"

He shook his head. "In Washington. I insisted on it. I didn't want the kids to have to pull up their roots every time I was transferred. Now I wish I'd kept them with me."

"You can keep them with you from now on."

He grinned at me. "Sure. Sure I can." But it was plain that he didn't believe he would ever see his family again. There was a sudden drawn, gray look about his face. Payne believed he was going to die.

I began to wonder if any of us would survive

this day. I wondered if I would ever see Bismarck or Dodge again and that made me think of Jennie and of the things that had led up to my meeting her.

All during the winter of '68 I drove a freight wagon between Fort Cobb and Dodge City on the Arkansas. But in the spring I signed on with a cattle herd heading up the trail to Dodge and when the trail crew went south to Texas after delivering the herd, I went along with them.

Covering forty or fifty miles a day, we traveled south. I had the promise of a job at Hat Ranch on the north bank of the Brazos, but I never got that far. I picked up the trail of a small band of Comanches and maybe out of sudden loneliness for my Indian friends, maybe just on impulse, I left the Hat cowhands and followed it.

Two days west I came upon a gutted, burned-out ranch. I found a dead white man there, stripped and scalped and mutilated and I found evidence that the Comanches had taken the woman who had lived here with him and at least one small child. The trail continued west.

I followed, marveling at my own foolishness. There were six Comanches in that raiding party. I was no match for six seasoned braves.

But the things I had learned from the Cheyenne now enabled me to slip up on the Comanche camp. The woman was not tied but it was plain she had been beaten and mistreated, things she had apparently endured for the sake of the small boy she had with her and of the baby she carried in her arms.

I waited patiently behind a rock fifty yards above their camp. I waited until all the light had faded from the sky, until the only light remaining down there was that cast by the dying fire in the middle of their camp. I knew I had to act pretty soon or back off because I had to have a little light by which to shoot.

I studied the woman carefully. She was tall and there was a gauntness about her common in ranch women of the plains. Her cheeks were hollow, her cheekbones prominent. Her eyes seemed sunken and her mouth, while full, was drawn now into a thin, determined line. I judged her to be about twenty-one or two. She looked twenty-five or six.

One of the Comanches spoke to her. I understood enough Comanche to know he was asking her for food, but she didn't understand. She looked at him uncomprehendingly.

He rose and came to the fire. He struck her a savage, backhanded blow that sent her staggering away. She fell awkwardly, trying to protect her baby as she fell. The little boy got to his feet and rushed at the Indian, who struck him too. The boy fell and did not move again.

I got mad. I put my sights on the Indian's chest and squeezed off my shot. The Indian was driven back toward the fire. He tripped at the edge of it and fell across it but he didn't cry out with pain because he was already dead.

I wasn't looking at him. Already I had a bead on the second of the six and I killed him the same way, instantly.

The remaining four melted into the darkness before I had a chance to shoot again. I knew they were on their way to where they'd seen my gun flash so I made tracks out of there mighty fast. I put fifty yards between me and that spot before I even stopped to listen.

There were sounds. There are always sounds out on the plain. I could hear the sound of wind rustling the grass. I could hear the woman sobbing softly by the fire and the whimpering of the baby in her arms. But suddenly there was another sound, very faint, the sound of moccasins in dry grass less than a dozen feet away from me.

Without thinking, I launched myself in that direction and collided violently with another of the Comanche braves.

This one was shorter by six inches than me, but heavyset and powerful. I slammed my gun stock squarely into his face, then reversed the direction of its swing and smashed the butt down on the top of his head.

I felt the give as the Indian's skull was crushed but I didn't wait for him to fall. I was already moving on, knowing the other three would head straight for the scuffling sounds we'd made.

Fifty feet farther on I stopped and stood motionless, hardly daring to breathe, listening again. A gun flashed less than twenty feet from me. The bullet grazed my rump and made me straighten up with a yell. But I was turning too and I fired before the flash of the Comanche's rifle had died away.

I didn't know whether I hit him or not. I didn't wait to see. I limped away into the darkness, hearing their guns boom out behind me, hearing the sound of one of their bullets striking the ground and ricocheting away.

I was even madder now because the rump is a

hell of a place to shoot a man. It hurt like hell and the seat of my pants was soaked with blood. It would be a long time before I could sit a saddle comfortably.

Three of the bucks, I was thinking, or four of them, were out of the fight, maybe even dead. From livin' with the Cheyenne, I understood the Indian mind pretty well. Right now they were figuring that their medicine was bad and they were anxious to get the hell out of here. But if they could, they'd kill the woman and her two little kids before they left because they blamed her for the fix they were in.

I ran toward the fire, as quietly as I could. I burst into the circle of firelight, wishing I could do this more gently but knowing I could not.

I struck her with my body, catching her in my arms as I did, and I kept right on going until we were clear of the firelight. I said, "I ain't going to hurt you, ma'am. You lie down on the ground and don't move or make a sound until I tell you it will be all right."

She made no sound to show that she had heard. But I could feel her trembling and I could feel how soft and warm she was. The baby made one small cry before she either put a hand over its mouth or brought its face against her body to muffle the tiny cry.

I left her and returned to the fire for the unconscious boy. Running, I scooped him up one handed even as a rifle flared less than a dozen yards away.

From the sound of it the rifle was an old one, probably smoothbore, probably a muzzle loader. And it sure as hell was empty now.

I dropped the boy and swerved in the direction from which the shot had come. Running, I covered the distance in seconds. I saw the blur in the darkness that was the Indian, slid to a halt and fired as soon as I was steady on my feet. I saw the Indian fall.

One left, I was thinking, but then I heard the rapid pound of hoofs fading into the night.

I waited until the sounds had completely died away. Then I called, "All right, ma'am. You can come to the fire now."

She didn't come. Instead I heard the awful sounds of her weeping from the darkness. They were harsh, tearing sounds that just went on and on and wouldn't stop. I walked toward the sounds and a little later reached her where she was still crouched down on the ground.

I stooped over and raised her up. I put my arms around her, not knowing what I ought to do or how to make her stop. The baby was crying too and I thought, Oh God, how the hell did I ever get myself into this? I'm shot in the ass and can't ride and now I've got a bellerin' woman and a couple of little kids to look after too.

I got loose from her and led her to where the fire was. I dragged the dead Indian out of it, hoping she hadn't noticed the smell of scorching flesh. I dragged the other Indian back into the darkness, then I built up the fire with the buffalo chips the Indians had gathered earlier. After that I went out and brought the boy in. He was coming back to consciousness and didn't seem to be hurt. Just stunned.

All this time I avoided turning my back to the woman because I didn't want her to see what had happened to me. That's a pretty humiliating place to get shot. But she did see and she made me come and drop my pants while she bandaged me with strips she tore from her ragged dress. My face was burning something fierce all the time she was doing it. A man doesn't like to feel a fool, but there didn't seem to be any help for it.

We pulled out in the darkness just in case that

Indian came back with some of his friends and we rode all night, her and the baby on one of the Indian horses, me on my own with the little boy in front of me. I had to keep my weight on the stirrups most of the time so by daylight I was ready to stop and rest. I led the horses down into a dry wash where they couldn't be seen and we all laid down and went to sleep, me with my stinking saddle blanket over me and her in my blanket with the two kids snuggled close to her.

When I woke up it was coming on dusk but there was still plenty of light to see. I stood looking down at her and those two kids sleeping so peacefully.

The bad time they'd had sure showed. There were tear streaks on the faces of all of them. But I got a funny feeling looking down at them. Like they were mine. Like they were part of me. The woman opened her eyes and looked up at me, as scared as if I was an Indian, and the feeling wasn't there any more.

XIV

DURING THE next hour and a half the men of the 7th bitterly cursed the sun, hanging so deliberately in the west, a glaring white ball shining through the overcast. There was a line of blue sky over the hills west of us and at last the sun slid from behind the clouds, bathing the land in direct sunlight for the first time today.

I knew the men were praying for darkness and I was praying for it myself. In darkness there would be rest, a respite from the hail of bullets and arrows that had rained on us all afternoon. There would be a chance to build fires and cook bacon and make coffee. There would be a chance for the men to sleep, however briefly. Indians will seldom attack at night. They believe the soul of a man killed at night forever wanders between earth and sky, belonging to neither one.

The sun finally went down, and the clouds flamed red in its dying glow. The red light cast upon the land was eerie, as though even the sun was bathing it with blood. It was a red Sabbath, dying now, but one that would never die in the memories of those of us who still remained alive. Provided we managed to stay live.

Red faded to purple and at last to gray. In the half light of dusk, the Sioux firing quickened, but as night crept across the land it finally slackened and stopped.

So great was the relief in the besieged position that here and there a young trooper wept, with nobody to criticize. Benteen did not allow the men to relax too much. Almost immediately a trumpeter blew officers call and the officers left their commands and walked to the center of the compound, to a place not far from where the wounded were. I walked along with Lieutenant Payne.

Reno was there and so was Benteen. Reno deferred to Benteen and the captain said, "We have come through the day, gentlemen, and we will come through the night. General Terry will be at the mouth of the Little Big Horn tomorrow. We will have to hold out tonight and tomorrow and perhaps tomorrow night. Tell your men they may build fires to make coffee if they can find anything that will burn, but tell them to stay out of the firelight as much as possible and to build small fires that will not give off much light."

He paused a moment. His white hair made a blur in the darkness. "Let them eat and rest for two hours. At the end of that time I want every available man put to work digging in. There will not be enough shovels to go around, so they are to use anything that comes to hand, knives, mess kits, anything. By dawn, I expect to see every man in this command protected by rifle pits and redoubts."

None of the assembled officers spoke. Benteen said, "That is all, gentlemen. Return to your commands."

I returned with Payne and Moylan to A Troop. Payne said, "Miles, you've got to get some sleep. You're not going to make it if you don't. There are plenty of men to work on the rifle pits. We don't need you."

I didn't argue with him. My strength had seemed to disappear when the sun went down. I'd kept going before that because I had to but I didn't have to any more. I laid down in a spot where I would be out of the way and closed my eyes.

My shoulder throbbed and so did the wound

along my ribs. My back burned where the tomahawk had grazed the skin. My head whirled.

I wondered what the country was going to
think of this. Custer was a war hero, a famous
Indian fighter, still popular with the people even if
he was in disfavor with his superiors and the Pres-
ident. His destruction would add to the flames of
hatred between Indians and whites. It could only
hasten the Indian's end.

I slept and it seemed only minutes before Lieutenant Payne touched me and spoke softly to
waken me. He said, "I've got some food and
coffee here for you, Miles. Do you feel like sitting
up to eat?"

I struggled to a sitting position, grimacing with
pain. Fires were burning here and there within our
perimeter, small fires that did not give off much
light. I could smell bacon and coffee and suddenly
I was ravenous. I took the plate and cup from
Payne and wolfed down the food. I drank the
coffee, thinking it was the best I had ever tasted in
my life. I could feel strength returning before I
had even finished it.

Nearby, the men of A Troop worked steadily,
digging in the rocky ground. Some carried empty
packs from the center of the compound to pile

atop the dead horse and mule carcasses that had been dragged up as redoubts.

I got to my feet and walked to a nearby fire to refill my coffee cup. I sipped coffee and stared out across the valley of the Little Big Horn toward the Indian villages in the distance northwest of us. Huge fires had been built all over the valley floor. Figures danced around the fires, looking like devils in the distance against the firelight. Faint came their cries on the light night breeze, faint and shrill and primitive.

The sounds of shovels, of mess kits and knives digging trenches were constant, busy sounds. Men talked softly among themselves. Tobacco smoke was a pleasant smell in the cool night air. I put down my cup and walked to the edge of the plateau.

There was a break here between the fortifications of K Troop and those of G. I caught a movement on the slope below . . .

I narrowed my eyes. Suddenly the shape was lighted faintly by firelight cast upward on the pall of valley dust. I was able to identify the shape as that of a trooper, not that of an Indian, and I yelled, "Hey!"

The man turned his head, then ducked it and

went on. I plunged down the slope after him. A recruit, I supposed, exhausted and terrified, trying in his terror to desert. He wouldn't get half a mile before the Sioux caught him. He didn't have a chance.

The slope was steep, brushy and littered with rocks. I stumbled once and nearly fell, wrenching my shoulder as I did. I could feel sweat spring out on my forehead from the pain. I wanted to yell at the man to stop but now I didn't dare. There could be Indians nearby keeping an eye on us to see that we did not move out during the night.

About fifty feet separated me from the deserter ahead of me. He reached the level valley floor and began to run upstream, away from the Sioux villages. I followed for a quarter mile before I dared call out to him. "Hey! Come back here! You haven't got a chance of getting through all these Indians!"

The figure stopped. I went on, more slowly, a little cautiously. If the man was desperate enough to desert he might also be desperate enough to try killing me.

A dozen feet away from him I stopped, my back to a high clump of brush. I said softly, "Don't be a fool. Come back with me. We can get inside the line without being seen and I won't open my mouth about what you tried to do."

"You can go straight to hell, Lorette."

I recognized the voice immediately. It was that of Nick Stavola. I said, "What's the matter with you? You know you can't get through all these Indians."

"The hell I can't!"

"They'll kill you."

"They'll kill me if I stay on that hill. When daylight comes, they're going to kill us all."

"You don't know that. We've held out so far. There's no reason to think we can't go on holding out until Terry and Gibbon come."

"I'll take my chances this way, Lorette. Go on back and leave me be or by God I'll stick this knife in you."

I didn't reply because I had heard something beyond Stavola and slightly to my right. Not a plain noise, hardly even a noise. Just something that sounded a warning in my Indian trained senses.

I froze, and waited, not speaking, hardly daring to breathe. I wanted to warn Stavola but I knew if I did I'd give us both away. He turned and blundered away, making as much noise as a cow elk in a thicket of dry scrub oak.

He had gone less than fifty feet before I saw half a dozen shadowy figures close with him. There was a brief flurry of movement, the sounds of scuffling feet and several grunts of exertion. Stavola's voice yelled, "Help, Lor . . . !" before it was cut off.

I remained with my back to the clump of brush. The fool, I thought. The damned stupid fool. Now they had him and if he wasn't dead I had to try getting him away from them.

The Indians were talking among themselves. I didn't understand the Sioux language well, but I knew a little of it. One of the bucks was telling the others that they'd better look around, that this pony soldier might not have been alone.

How far would they look, I wondered, and how thoroughly? I gripped my revolver butt with one hand, thumb on the hammer, but left it in the holster for fear that even the slight noise I made drawing it would give my presence away. I held my breath as they fanned out in all directions to look.

One came toward me, straight toward me. I'd have to kill him if he got close enough to see me and then make a run for it, I thought. But I didn't dare use the gun. A gunshot would bring a hundred of them down on me.

I put my left hand on the handle of my knife. My sleeve brushed against my buckskin shirt, making the slightest of whispering sounds.

The Sioux froze, listening, but when the sound was not repeated, he came toward me again.

I don't know what would have happened if right then some buck out in the valley hadn't begun shooting into the air with a revolver taken earlier from one of the dead officers. The one approaching me grunted something and turned back toward the others and I let my breath sigh out silently.

Talking excitedly among themselves, they carried Stavola away. I followed, as quietly as any Indian. They headed toward a fire not more than a quarter mile away.

One of them called out to those at the fire as they approached. The others came running out and swarmed around the six as they carried Stavola into the firelight.

They threw him down and immediately began to strip off his clothes. One already wore his hat. Another now put on his tunic. Still another put on his pants. A fourth put on his underwear and began to cavort around the fire with it, making obscene gestures and howling with laughter. He was so comical that I had to grin, but the grin didn't stay on my face very long, because one of the Indians pulled his knife and walked toward Stavola.

I had five bullets in my revolver. I was thinking I could get five of them but even if I did, there would still be five left. And Stavola wasn't conscious. He couldn't travel and I couldn't carry him.

I didn't like Stavola. I never had. But I'd have tried to rescue him in spite of that if it had been possible. It wasn't possible. I could only do one thing for him. If they started to torture him, I'd put him out of his misery and then try to get away myself. I figured I could move as quietly as any Indian here. I'd have better than an even chance of making it safely back.

Grinning, the Indian with the knife knelt beside Stavola. I saw what he was going to do and I knew after he did it Stavola wouldn't want to live, even if he somehow managed to get away. I took careful aim and put a bullet into Stavola's head.

Before the roar of the gun had died from my ears I was moving, running, not toward the hill where the 7th was but straight away from it. I figured they'd look for me first between the fire and the hill and I was right. Howling, they plunged away, straight toward the hill, straight toward the spot where I'd been when I shot Stavola.

I stopped and waited several moments until I was sure one of them hadn't hung back. There was nothing further I could do for Stavola. He was dead. Not that he'd ever had anything better than death to look forward to once he'd left his company on the hill. If I hadn't killed him the Sioux would have done it.

But I was alive and I intended to stay that way if it was possible. I headed upstream, toward the south, moving slowly and with extreme care. I had all night to get back on that hill. If I tried hurrying I might not get back at all.

I traveled south for half a mile before I cut back into the hills. After that I turned north again, staying high, moving slow, as carefully as a cat. It was past midnight before I came within hailing distance of the sentries on the knoll where the 7th was digging in.

When I figured it was safe, I called out and after a little talk back and forth succeeded in identifying myself, to the sentry's satisfaction and he let me come in. Benteen was there and he asked me where I'd been. I told him but I didn't tell him I'd killed Stavola. He had enough to worry about without worrying about whether he ought to hold me for the murder of one of his men.

Walking toward the place I'd left Payne and A Troop, I ran into Reno. He was talking to Lieutenant Edgerly, who had apparently just wakened. Reno's voice was unbelieving as he said, "Great God, man, I don't see how you can sleep!"

He had my sympathy. Command weighed heavily on him. He felt responsible for all that had happened to his men.

But if there was responsibility, if there was blame, it should be laid where it belonged. This whole miserable mess was Custer's fault. If he hadn't been so greedy, if his thirst for glory had not been so overpowering, this could not have happened at all.

XV

WHEN I reached A Troop, Payne came to me immediately. He said, "Who was it?"

"Who was who?"

"The man you went out after. The deserter."

"I didn't know him."

"Liar."

I grinned at him. "What difference would it make? He's dead."

"None I guess. It was Stavola, wasn't it?"

I didn't reply.

"Was he trying to get to Custer or trying to get away?"

"Why would he try to get to Custer?"

"To kill him. Stavola hated him."

I said, "I'm tired, Lieutenant. Let's forget it. The deserter is dead, whoever he was."

"All right, Miles. I guess it doesn't matter anyway."

"You sound like you thought we all were going to die."

"Aren't we?"

"Hell no, we aren't. I agree with Benteen. Terry and Gibbon are on the way. Crook might show up any time."

"Crook is overdue. And what if Terry and Gibbon have been jumped by the Sioux? What if they're pinned down the way we are?"

"It's not likely. They weren't even supposed to reach the mouth of the Little Big Horn until tomorrow, and with all the Sioux in this valley it's doubtful if they have villages anyplace else. Huh uh. The odds are that Gibbon and Terry are all right and that they're on the way."

"Even if they are, the Sioux still outnumber them."

"You're worn out, Lieutenant. You need some sleep. You're looking on the dark side of everything."

He made a thin smile. "I suppose I am." He stared closely at me. There was not much light, only a little cast by a small fire nearby and by the stars, but I could see his face and I suppose he could see mine. He asked, "How do you keep going, Miles? You're wounded but you've been doing as much as anyone."

"I'm practically an Indian myself. I think like

they do and I've learned it does no good to think about how much you hurt or how tired you are."

"If you think like they do, tell me what they're going to do when it gets light."

"They're going to hit us with everything they've got. They'll keep on hitting us until they figure the cost is getting too damned high. Then they'll quit. When they start losing too many men, Indians figure their medicine is bad and they pull back to wait for a day when it's good again."

"I hope you're right."

He left me and walked the length of the defense line assigned to A Troop. It was not very long. A Troop's casualties had been terrible, both in the grove and up here during the retreat from the promontory to which Weir and Edgerly had gone. I could still hear the clinking sounds of the men digging in the rocky ground. A Troop had no shovels but they had knives and mess kits and they had been working diligently with these. Already they had a trench over a foot in depth. The loose dirt had been piled in front of it, and they were continuing to work. By morning the trench would be two feet deep, with perhaps another foot and a half of dirt piled up in front. The first of the attacking Sioux were going to get a surprise. They would find very little of each man exposed.

I sat down and put my back against one of the mule packs. I fumbled for a cigar and lighted it. I was tired and my shoulder hurt, but I knew I was going to make it, at least through tonight and tomorrow, provided I did not get shot again. I let myself think of Jennie and closed my eyes, trying to remember her face and the way she smiled.

I opened my eyes and saw Private Overby looking down at me. He seemed to want to say something, but was hesitant. At last he said, "Mr. Lorette—you were down in the valley a little while ago, weren't you?"

"Uh huh. Why?"

"I was wondering . . . Did you see any sign of the general?"

"I didn't go that way. I was trying to bring a deserter back."

"Nick?"

"How did you know?"

"He said he was going to desert."

I said, "I think the general is dead."

"I hope to God he is. I just hope to God he is."

He stood there, shifting from one foot to the other. He didn't seem to want to leave. Neither did he seem to know what to say. I said, "I heard

you sounding off about the war one time in the
sutler's store at Fort Lincoln. Custer hanged your
father, didn't he?"

"Yes, sir. It was murder but he got away with
it." He squatted down suddenly. His shoulders
had begun to shake. In a voice hardly louder than
a whisper, he said, "I was going to kill him. When
we went into action, I was going to get behind him
and shoot him in the back. That's what he
deserved. My father was a regular, Mr. Lorette.
He wasn't a spy and he wasn't a guerrilla. He was
a regular in the Confederate Cavalry but Custer
hanged him like he was a criminal or a spy."

"Why?"

Private Overby said bitterly, "Because we were
beating him, that's why. Colonel Mosby beat him
pretty near every time he turned around. This one
time, though, Mosby attacked a Union train
coming into Front Royal and he got driven off.
My pa and five others were captured. Custer had
four of them shot while his damned band played
the dead march and then he hanged my pa and
another man from a tree right there in the middle
of town in front of everybody. He even pinned a
sign on my pa's tunic saying that would be the fate
of all Mosby's gang."

I didn't say anything because there was nothing I could say. Overby had simply wanted to get the story off his chest. He stood up. "Thanks for listening, Mr. Lorette. I feel better now. I guess I've carried this around for a long, long time. Maybe too long. Anyway, I'm glad I don't have to kill him. Maybe I wouldn't have been able to do it when the time came."

I said, "Time tends to cool a man's hate. I hated Custer once and wanted to kill him for what he did at the Washita. But I wouldn't have killed him any more than you would."

Overby stared down at me soberly. "I've wished him dead a thousand times, I guess, but I didn't want anybody else to die with him. You don't think me wishing him dead had anything to do with what happened, do you?"

"Don't give yourself too much importance, Overby. What would the wishes of a private have to do with what happens to a general?"

He nodded. "I'd better get back to work." He walked away and disappeared into the darkness. I closed my eyes and was almost instantly asleep.

It was an uneasy sleep, filled with unpleasant dreams. I went through the Sand Creek massacre again, and rode up the valley of the Washita again, and killed the Comanches that had kidnapped Jennie and her kids again.

I woke up sweating and shaking with a chill. I got up and walked to the nearest fire. I hunkered down close and spread my hands to it. My shoulder had stiffened so that it was difficult to move at all, but I figured it would loosen up if I kept moving around between now and the time that it got light.

Herendeen, the scout Gibbon had loaned Custer, came and squatted beside me. He asked, "How's the shoulder, Miles?"

I shrugged, then winced. "It'll be all right."

He said, "You and me are about all that's left. Reynolds got it down there in the grove and Bouyer was with Custer."

I said, "And the Crows and Arikaras are gone. They flew the coop the minute things began to look rough. Except for Bloody Knife. I even ran into one of the Crows driving a herd of stolen Sioux horses south. I wonder if he got away with it."

Herendeen grinned. "If he did, he'll never quit talking about it. Not that I'd blame him much. Stealing Sioux horses out of this valley under the noses of thousands of them would be quite a thing."

"How far away do you think Gibbon and Terry are?"

"They'll be at the mouth of the Little Horn tomorrow. Unless they get jumped too."

"And how long do you figure it will take them to get to us? You know this part of the country a lot better than I do."

"A day and a night, maybe, depending on how much trouble the Sioux give them."

I said softly, "We could all get wiped out the way Custer likely was. Gibbon and Terry too."

"We could but I doubt if we will. The Sioux jumped Custer and us because we were heading toward their villages to attack. If Terry and Gibbon don't attack 'em, I figure the Indians will let them alone. And both Terry and Gibbon have got better sense than to attack now with no more men than they've got left."

That made sense. Terry and Gibbon were old hands, not glory hunting fools like Custer. Herendeen said, "I happen to have a little nip cached away in one of the mule packs. Care to join me?"

I nodded, got to my feet and followed him to the center of the horseshoe-shaped defense perimeter. He rummaged in one of the packs and came up with a brown bottle. He uncorked it and handed it to me. I took a drink and handed it back. He drank, replaced the cork, then put the bottle back into the pack.

I glanced up at the stars. It would be getting light soon, I thought, and as soon as it was light enough the Sioux would attack again.

I said, "Smells like rain."

Herendeen nodded.

Out in the valley, suddenly, a trumpet blew the charge. The notes were clear and plain, if faint with distance.

For a full minute every sound within the compound stopped. It was as though the men stopped breathing. Even the wounded were silent, listening . . .

And then, as suddenly as they had fallen silent, the men shouted with relief. Some yelled, "It's Terry! He's here!"

Herendeen was frowning. So was I. Both of us knew Terry couldn't possibly have gotten here this soon. Was it Custer then? Was he still alive? Was he leading a charge to our relief?

I shook my head. Excited talk ran the length and breadth of our besieged position. Some of the men were laughing hysterically. Some were weeping unashamedly.

Benteen saw Herendeen and me and came hurrying to us. He looked puzzledly at Herendeen. "What is it? Could it be Terry? This soon?"

Herendeen shook his head. "No, Captain. It ain't Terry. I'll take an oath on that."

"Then who? Custer? Could he be alive and trying to join up with us? Or could it be Crook?"

All of us were peering out toward the valley, trying to pierce the darkness, trying desperately to see. No sound of galloping hoofs came on the heels of the bugle call. No wild yells.

Suddenly the solemn notes of taps were sounded out where the charge had been blown only minutes before. "That's an Injun blowin' a horn taken from one of Custer's trumpeters," I said.

Herendeen said, "That's sure as hell what it is."

"But how . . ." Benteen stopped when he realized that there was no reason a Sioux couldn't know the cavalry bugle calls. There was no reason why one of them couldn't be proficient with the instrument.

A stunned silence hung over the besieged plateau, lasting two, three times as long as had the first silence only moments before. A murmuring began to grow among the men as they began to understand. Terry was not out there in the valley with his command nor was Crook. It was a cruel trick being played by a Sioux who happened to know the bugle calls.

Murmuring grew to an angry roar. Men stood up and shook their fists at the dark valley where the Indians were. They cursed at the top of their voices, hurling the vilest words they knew at the bugler.

Benteen turned and roared, "It's only a Sioux blowing a captured horn! Get back to work. In another hour we'll need every bit of protection we can get!"

Grumbling and sullen, the men went back to work. I looked at Herendeen. "That buck was just having some fun with a horn he took from one of Custer's trumpeters. He didn't have any idea what effect it would have on the men up here. But if he'd thought about it a week he couldn't have come up with anything that would discourage these men any more than that."

I glanced toward the east. Yesterday at this time we had been at the foot of the Crow's Nest, waiting for it to get light enough to see. Now a line of gray was beginning to silhouette the jagged line of mountains there. Half an hour, I thought. In half an hour it would be light enough for the

Sioux to mount their dawn attack.

I walked slowly toward A Troop's position on the edge of the plateau. I was tired, and discouraged, and without much hope. I wondered if all the men felt as gloomy as I did about our prospects of getting out of this alive. Almost as if it would provide a link between me and life, which seemed to be slipping away, I began thinking about Jennie again.

Jennie thought of me as wild, I guess. She'd been married to a farming man who had never killed anyone, not even when the Comanche raiding party hit their ranch and killed him and kidnapped her and the kids. She'd seen the way I jumped those six bucks and killed five of them and while she was grateful to me for getting her and the kids away, she was still scared of me. I guess my face isn't too pretty when I'm in a fight. It's not exactly pretty any time.

We angled northeast and when we struck the Arkansas we followed it to Dodge. She sent a telegram to her father in St. Louis and then went to the hotel. She thanked me with tears in her eyes but I somehow got the idea she didn't particularly want to see me again.

My wound was festering so I went to the doctor to get it fixed. He was a little drunk and he sure did hurt me while he was cleaning and rebandaging it, but he didn't laugh or snicker about where it was. And he didn't say a damn word as he unwrapped those strips torn from Jennie's petticoat. It's a good thing he didn't. I was feeling proddy by that time.

I paid him and left and went into the first saloon I came to and got a bottle and a glass. Somehow or other I just couldn't get Jennie off my mind. I drank half the bottle but I still didn't get so drunk I couldn't manage to get around. All the time, her face was there in my mind and wouldn't go away.

I left, finally, and went down to the telegraph office. I don't know what got into me, doing it, but I wanted to see her again, even if it was only to take the answer to her telegram up to her.

I'd been with her when she sent the telegram so the operator didn't question me when I asked if there was a reply. He just gave it to me and I went out with it.

As soon as I was around the corner I stopped and unfolded it. I read it, ashamed of myself for snooping, but telling myself maybe I had the right.

It said her father was dead. I took the telegram to the hotel and up to her room She came to the door and I handed it to her. She read it and began to cry and I wanted to put my arms around her but I didn't because I was afraid to push.

She stopped crying after a while. The two kids were sleeping on the bed. She'd given them a bath. The wooden tub was still there in the middle of the floor.

She started asking me questions about whether she could sell her ranch and her cattle and I told her that the way things were nobody would want the place. I said with the Comanche on the warpath it'd even be hard to get men to go down there and round her cattle up unless she could give them some kind of guarantee. I asked if her father had left her anything and she said no, he didn't have anything to leave.

I said I'd see what I could do and she said she was already in my debt and I said forget it and went on out. There were still a few Texas cowhands in town so I talked to some of them. They just laughed at me. That ranch of hers, they said, was right at the edge of the Llano Estacado, which was the Comanche stronghold and the Indians were still stirred up over that business on the Washita.

I went back to the hotel and told her what had happened. I said maybe if she'd offer shares to the men willing to go gather her cattle up, I could get someone crazy enough to try. It was like saying I was crazy enough because I was going along to make sure they didn't steal her blind whether I got a share or not.

She said yes, to offer whatever shares I had to. I went back and made the round of the saloons again, offering five percent shares to anybody that would go. I got six who would.

All six were trail hands up from Texas. They were hardcases and looked like they'd be able to take care of themselves no matter what came up. We didn't have the kind of outfit we ought to have had because there was no money for outfitting. But we each had a horse, a rifle, a revolver and a lot of ammunition for both. Each of us had a blanket roll and a slicker and some salt and coffee and bacon and a cook outfit. We figured to live off the country or off her beef if there wasn't any other way.

When we were all ready to go, I went up to her room at the hotel. I said it might be several weeks before we got back, depending on how much trouble we ran into and how the weather was. She said she'd got a job in the hotel working as a chambermaid. It would pay for her room and for food for herself and the kids. I was about to give her what money I had left but I didn't because I suddenly saw from her expression that she regretted the way she was already in debt to me. For the first time I felt irritated with her for that, but I got over it right away.

I went back downstairs and mounted up and we rode south out of town. I looked back as we were leaving the hotel and saw her and the little boy in the window waving their hands at me.

XVI

THERE WAS an air of tension, of expectancy in the trenches facing the valley of the Little Big Horn as light crept across the sky. The trenches and redoubts protected the men from bullets fired up at them from the valley floor and from the lower ridges fingering into the valley on left and right but they did not protect the men from snipers in the higher country at the rear.

It was almost a relief when the first rifle cracked. And as though that first Sioux rifle shot had been a signal, others opened up suddenly on all sides of us.

I could faintly see the valley floor as the light grew stronger in the leaden sky. A man next to me straightened and fell backward, blood spurting from his mouth. Another trooper yelled for the surgeon but it was too late. The man was dead.

Captain Moylan roared, "Make your bullets count. It'll take more than noise to scare 'em off!"

I felt a drop of moisture on my face. I glanced up and another drop touched my face. It had begun to rain, softly, gently, almost silently. A curtain of rain now marched across the valley floor, first covering the brown tipis of the Indian villages and the temporary wickiups, then sweeping toward our position and enveloping it.

It was warm rain, and light, but once it had soaked the men's clothes the wind that came with it chilled them and set them to shivering. A few scurried away to get slickers from their horses. Others hunched down into upturned collars and stared gloomily at the Indian horde milling around on the valley floor out of rifle range.

Nearer, every clump of brush concealed an Indian, who fired through it so that all we could see was the puff of smoke.

I got out of the trench and, hunched over, hurried toward the place I had left my horse. I was cold from the rain and wind. I was shivering violently as though I had a chill. I realized that I was feverish from my wounds and would go on shivering until I got warm, until I got dry again.

There was a blazing fire near where the wounded were. There were two large iron kettles suspended over it. One contained about an inch of bloody boiling water in which were the surgeon's instruments. The other had a little coffee in it. I stopped and hunkered down close to the blaze.

Dr. Porter worked steadily, tirelessly. He glanced at me as he passed the fire, but he didn't speak. He seemed oblivious of the bullets thudding into the compound, of the arrows raining down. One bullet struck the fire in front of me and raised a shower of sparks. I ducked away involuntarily.

A man was moaning softly. Another, a mere boy, wept. Still another shouted with pain and interspersed his shouts with curses, at Custer, at the Sioux, at the Army and the 7th Cavalry. Nobody paid any attention to him or tried to quiet him.

My clothes were steaming and I was beginning to feel warm again. My shivering gradually grew less, and finally stopped. I got up and walked among the horses until I found my own. I got my slicker from the back of the saddle and put it on.

The horses were terrified. One broke loose from the picket line, an arrow sticking in his rump. He began to buck, as though trying to dislodge it. He bucked across the compound, plowed through one of the trenches, scattered men to left and right, then ran down the hill and into the milling throng of Indians.

A sergeant roared, "Smith! Bronson! Stotts! Get over there and calm them damned horses down!"

The three he had named ran to help those already trying to calm the horses, well aware that if the horses got away the command's chance of survival would be reduced.

With my slicker on, I returned to A Troop's trench and slid into it beside Lieutenant Payne. The shower had stopped but I could see another marching up the valley a mile away.

I saw a Sioux stick his head out on one side of a clump of brush. Smoke puffed from the muzzle of his gun. I raised my rifle and fired instantly. He straightened but before he could fall, two more bullets slammed into him, fired by troopers farther down the trench. He rolled down the slope for ten or fifteen feet before he stopped. He didn't move again.

Turning my head, I saw Benteen and Reno talking with the surgeon near the fire where I had warmed myself a few minutes earlier. Reno beckoned a huge, red-haired sergeant and said something to him. A moment later the sergeant called several men from a trench and they began working their way along the trenches, collecting canteens.

That meant the command was short of water, I thought. Kegs of water carried on the mules had either been used up or lost or punctured by Sioux bullets. We were down to what was left in the men's canteens and I doubted if that was going to be very much.

I hadn't thought about it before, but I suddenly realized how thirsty I was. I stared at the men around me. All of them were licking their lips as though suddenly thinking about water now that they knew it was in short supply.

The wounded were going to get all the water remaining, I thought. The rest of the men would have to do without. But I didn't see a single man drink from his canteen before surrendering it.

Loading down with canteens, the sergeant and the men he had detailed to help made their way to the fire and dumped them on the ground. . . .

A sudden yipping in the direction of the bluff brought my glance around. Down the ridge came a galloping wave of Indians, yelling, firing, waving their weapons in the air.

Benteen roared something I didn't hear, but it wasn't necessary to hear. All of us knew what to do.

Those in the front of the horseshoe and some of those on the sides had to hold their fire temporarily for fear of hitting the horses, the wounded, or their own men farther along the trench. The wave of Sioux came on. . . .

The red-haired sergeant bawled, "Stay with them horses! Hold onto 'em!"

The line of galloping Indians were now within easy carbine range. More guns crackled up and down the line of trenches. There must be two or three hundred Indians in that line, I thought. They were five or six deep and the line was long enough to bend completely around our horseshoe-shaped line of defense.

The line struck the open end of the horseshoe. It bent, with the wings of the line continuing. The Indians in the center bunched and came straight into the horseshoe toward the horses and the wounded men.

The troopers in the trenches turned, firing point blank into the mounted horde of Indians. Horses fell, somersaulting and rolling. Indians were literally driven from their saddles, to sprawl upon the ground.

The men detailed to guard the horses ran to form a line between them and the Indians, kneeling, firing steadily.

Trapped, the Indian horses milled, caught between the two ends of the horseshoe and the men guarding the picket line. More of them went down. Their riders wheeled and galloped them back in the direction from which they had come only a minute or two before.

They left half a dozen dead, as many wounded on the ground when they withdrew. Immediately, troopers moved in and savagely clubbed the Indian wounded with their rifle butts.

Around the sides of the defense perimeter, the

skirmish continued. The Indian line swept on, surrounding us. Other Indians from the valley galloped up the slope or ran up afoot.

A dozen young bucks rode their horses over
the barricades and down into the trenches. Others
followed them. In the center of the horseshoe,
Reno stared at the red tide sweeping over the
command with horror and dismay.

Benteen's voice overrode the noise. He stood
beside Reno, prompting the demoralized major,
issuing orders for the defense himself when Reno
failed to issue them himself, waving his long-bar-
reled revolver, yelling ferociously.

I had no time for more than a glance at him.
He had lost his hat. His white hair was in disarray,
both from rain and wind. He had a two-day
growth of whiskers on his ruddy face. He was covered with dust turned to mud by rain and there
was blood on his tunic front.

I yanked my head around. An Indian horse
leaped over the barricade and came straight down at
me. I threw myself aside, felt his hoof graze my head,
then rolled and fired up at the Sioux riding him.

The Indian was driven from the saddle by the
bullet's impact but he wasn't dead. He struck the
ground beyond the trench. Up almost immedi-

ately, he came charging back at me, steel tomahawk in his hand.

His face was twisted with effort and with pain.
For an instant I saw myself in him as I had been
after the Sand Creek killing, hating whites and
fighting back angrily. . . .

The tomahawk swung savagely as the Sioux
closed with me. I fired point-blank, my carbine
muzzle almost touching him.

His body slammed against me, the tomahawk
barely missing me. Both of us went down in the
bottom of the trench.

I struggled to get free. There was weight to the
Indian, but there was no life. He was limp. I rolled
him away and got to my knees.

Another Sioux horse came scrambling over the
barricade. I glimpsed Lieutenant Payne crouched
ten or fifteen feet away. His revolver was in his
hand. He fired and powdersmoke made a cloud in
front of him.

He pulled the trigger again but his gun clicked
on an empty chamber. He turned away to try and
reload. A Sioux buck on foot climbed over the
barricade and leaped at him, a knife fisted in his
hand.

I raised my Spencer and fired, knowing if it was

empty, Payne was dead. The gun fired and the bullet spun the Sioux halfway around. He did not drop the knife, but turned back toward Payne with it still clutched in his hand.

Payne slammed his revolver muzzle squarely into the Indian's face. The man went back. I clawed toward him and, reaching him, brought my rifle butt slamming down against his head.

I didn't know how the rest of the command was faring, I didn't have time to look. Indians kept coming over the barricade. The men of A Troop met them as they came, killing, sometimes dying or sustaining wounds themselves.

How long it continued, I have no idea. It seemed like hours. It was probably no more than five minutes at the most. I know that if the Sioux had kept up that kind of pressure another few minutes, they would have won. We could not have withstood it many minutes more.

But they did not keep the pressure up. Their losses had been too great. They stopped coming over the barricades. Their horsemen withdrew to the valley floor.

They left a shambles behind them within our horseshoe-shaped defense perimeter. Indian horses lay kicking everywhere. Dead and wounded Indians and dead and wounded troopers were scattered about impartially. Benteen roared. "I want a mop-up squad from each troop. Get rid of these damned wounded Indians before they kill any more of us."

Men piled out of the trenches, two or three from every troop. They moved among the litter of bodies, finishing off wounded Indians with their carbine butts, carrying their own wounded comrades to the fire where the other wounded were.

Two troopers drove a team of mules to the dead Indian horses, hitched chains onto them one by one, and dragged them away. If a horse was only wounded, they cut his throat, not wanting to waste a bullet on a horse.

Another squall of rain struck, sweeping coldly across the compound, heavier than before. It brought with it a fresh smell of damp grass and earth that temporarily obscured the smell of blood and powdersmoke and death.

Near me a man muttered, "Holy Jesus Christ, I thought we was done for that time. Another few minutes and we would of been done for too."

I sank back weakly against the muddy side of the trench. I could feel the warmth of blood on my bandages. Exertion had opened both wounds and started them bleeding again.

Payne walked along the trench to me. "Are you all right?"

I nodded, grinning as convincingly as I could. I had no intention of lying helplessly with the other wounded as long as I could get around. I wanted to be able to defend myself. Payne said, "You don't look very good."

"Neither do you. In fact you look like hell."

He squatted beside me and fished out a couple of crumpled, wet cigars. He offered me one and I stuck it into my mouth. He finally found a match that would light and touched it to the end of my cigar, afterward lighting up his own. He said, "I wonder where the hell Crook is."

"Probably got whipped by the Indians. We followed four hundred lodges up the Rosebud from the south. That bunch probably fought him and drove him back."

Payne nodded. He took off his hat and scratched his head. "And Terry can't possibly get here before tomorrow. I don't know whether we can hold out that long. Another charge like that last one . . ."

"The Indians got hurt in that last charge too. They lost a damn sight more men than we did."

"They've got more men to lose."

"But they don't like it any better than we do."

"No, I suppose not. What do you think they'll do now?"

"Pull back and lick their wounds. Put snipers behind every rock and clump of brush. They'll have a pow wow in the meantime to decide what they're going to do."

Somewhere a man began to beg for water. Another screamed in agony as the surgeon worked over him. Payne said, "We're out of water and we're damned near out of food." He looked longingly at the river twisting back and forth across the valley floor. "We should have sent men down after water last night while it was dark."

I nodded. Nobody had been thinking about water last night. Nobody had even realized we were almost out of it. But without water the wounded were going to suffer terribly. I knew from my own personal experience how horribly thirsty a wounded man can get.

XVII

As THOUGH angered by their losses and by the failure of their reckless charge, the Sioux now poured concentrated rifle fire into our position on the hill. Arrows, fired upward at a steep angle to give them maximum range, dropped like hail. Three men were hit by falling arrows in a matter of minutes. One of them, already wounded, died from the arrow, which pierced his chest.

Crouched in our trenches and behind our barricades, we waited out the deadly rain of arrows and of lead. Benteen strode back and forth restlessly, yelling at the men to keep down, apparently oblivious of the bullets thudding into the ground near to him. Sergeant Madden called, "Captain, sir, you tell us to keep down but it's yourself that should keep down. They'll get you, sure."

Benteen turned his head and grinned. "Pshaw. They can't hit me."

I raised my head cautiously and stared over the dead horse barricade immediately in front of me.

The horse's body was soaked from the rain and there was the smell of wet hair in the trench. It combined with the smell of wet sagebrush on the hillside, crushed by the recent Indian charge. The Sioux were now wriggling up the slope, taking cover where it was available, firing as rapidly as they could reload. In its way, I thought this advance was more deadly than the reckless charge of horsemen had been but both had the same goal. The Sioux intended to overrun our position. They meant to kill us down to the last remaining man.

And we couldn't just lie still here and wait. We had to do something and do it quick. I saw Benteen hurry to where Reno was. The two talked urgently. Reno seemed more restrained than did Benteen. At one point Benteen shouted something but the racket of rifle fire kept me from hearing what it was. At last Reno nodded and Benteen seized a horse's reins, mounted and rode to the trench where his own H Troop was.

He shouted at them and they left the trench and ran to the picket line. Benteen rode across the compound to where Captain French and M Troop were. He beckoned to them and they piled out of their trench and followed the men of H to the picket line.

Swiftly the troopers found their horses, mounted and formed company lines where Benteen and French were waiting for them. Another charge, I thought, to clear the slopes of snipers. It was dangerous but it was the only way to keep the Sioux from overrunning our position as soon as enough of them got close. A charge of cavalry would get them up from behind the rocks and brush concealing them. It would put them to flight back down the hill.

Benteen waved his revolver and shouted an order. H Troop followed him to the rear of the horseshoe-shaped defense perimeter. French's M Troop followed.

A couple of horses were hit and immediately exchanged. The two troops reached the rear of the horseshoe.

I could see both Benteen and French yelling but because of the racket, I couldn't hear their words. I knew what they had been, however, when the two troops spurred their horses forward, swung left and charged along the slope, the way Godfrey's fifteen men had yesterday.

The line was longer than Godfrey's had been, long enough to reach all the way to the foot of the hill and beyond. It was enormously effective as it

swept along. Ahead of the charging, yelling cavalrymen, Indians leaped to their feet and scurried
down the slope, some turning to fire as they ran,
some apparently with empty guns.

In the trenches, the troopers raised up and
fired at the running, retreating Sioux. A few went
down, but most reached the bottom of the hill.
The galloping line passed and as it did the men
ceased firing.

The line made the complete circle of our position and returned to the rear of the horseshoe.
The men rode inside, yelling to each other jubi-
lantly, their weariness and discouragement temporarily forgotten in the excitement of the charge.

They dismounted and returned their horses to
the picket line. They returned to the trenches they
had left only minutes earlier. For the first time
today, the Indians' firing slackened to an occasional shot from some distant, hidden rifleman.

In the lull, I began thinking of Jennie again, and
remembered the way she had looked waving down
to me from her hotel window as I rode south to try
gathering up her cattle. With me rode the six
others to whom I had promised shares.

It was a long, hard, grueling ride into the heart

of the Comanche stronghold where her ranch was located. We traveled at night and holed up by day. The six with me played cards a lot and considerable money changed hands between them. I stayed on guard because I wanted to keep my hair and get back to Jennie if possible. I'd admitted to myself that I was in love with her and wanted to marry her, although it was hard for me to convince myself that she would ever want to marry me.

We finally reached her burned-out ranch and set up camp. The first thing we did was to kill a calf so that we could eat. One of the men was detailed as camp cook and guard and the rest of us started building a corral out of mesquite.

I left the others to their corral building and rode out to scout. I made a big circle ten miles across without finding any Indian horse tracks fresher than three or four weeks.

We worked fast and hard, from first daylight until dark. We didn't get anywhere near all Jennie's cattle but we got about fifteen hundred head. Three weeks after we arrived, we started back toward Dodge, driving them ahead of us.

I had noticed something funny about the way the six looked at me and kept my eyes peeled for trouble. I figured they'd decided they weren't going to take five percent shares when they could each get a sixth of the herd by killing me.

We were well out of Comanche territory and across the Red River before they figured they didn't need me anymore. They waited until they thought I was asleep and then moved in on me in the darkness, the three who had been night herding standing back with rifles in case I got up and got away, one of the others with a handful of gun powder to throw on the fire to give them light to shoot by, the other two moving in with their knives to where they thought I was sleeping.

I'd been expecting something like this as soon as we crossed the Red so I'd left my bed earlier, filling it with buffalo chips to make it look like I was still there. I heard them cussing when they found they'd stuck their knives into a pile of old buffalo chips, and then the powder lighted up the camp long enough for me to drop two of the three standing there with rifles in their hands.

I changed position right away, while they blasted away at the flashes from my gun. I came in on the other side, quietly, the way I'd learned to move when I was with the Cheyenne. I put my knife in a third of the six and smashed the skull of the fourth with the barrel of my gun. The other two lost interest in the proceedings and hightailed it as fast as they could ride.

That left me out in the middle of nowhere with fifteen hundred head of cattle to try and drive all by myself. I knew I was going to lose some of them but as long as I didn't have to give anybody shares, maybe I'd still get to Dodge with as many as Jennie would have gotten out of it originally.

I stayed up all that night riding around the herd to keep it quiet, figuring the two who had got away might still come back and try starting a stampede. They didn't, though, and in the morning I trailed the herd out, along with the horses of the four dead men who sure wouldn't be needing them any more. I had to change horses pretty often, but I held the herd together and kept them moving fast enough and hard enough so that when I stopped at dark they were glad to lie down and rest. I kept going this way until I came to a ranch three days south of Dodge and was able to hire the rancher and his sons to help.

We got the herd to Dodge all right and I gave the rancher his pick of the herd, twenty head in all, for the help he'd given me. I took him up to Jennie's room at the hotel and told her to give him a bill of sale.

As soon as he had gone she asked me what had become of the six herders I took south with me. I told her I'd killed four of them when they tried to kill me and that the other two had got away.

I should have kept my damn mouth shut. Jennie's face got white and she looked at me as if I was some kind of monster or something. She said she guessed I was a wild Indian through and through and that I'd always be a savage, wouldn't I? I was getting mad by then and I said she was probably right, but where the hell would she and her two kids be if I hadn't come along and killed the Comanche bucks that had kidnapped her? Or where would she be if I'd just laid still and let those six men kill me and take her cattle for themselves?

She told me that wasn't the point and said I couldn't live like an Indian any more. I was a white man and had to live like white men did, by law. I asked her if that was the way those six had been living and her face got red and she said that was different and did I want to be like those six myself? I told her I just wanted to stay alive and that I intended to stay that way no matter what I had to do.

It was quite a fight we had, with the little boy

looking on scared and the baby crying because the yelling frightened him. I finally stomped out and she yelled after me that she'd have my share of the herd money put into the bank for me. I yelled back not to bother because I didn't want it anyway.

I got blind drunk and spent the night in one of the cribs but nothing helped. I rode out the next morning wondering where the hell I was going and how I was going to live if the Indians didn't want me and if I couldn't learn to live the way the whites were supposed to live. I didn't know if I'd ever be able to forget Jennie but I knew I had to try. I blundered into Fort Dodge, a few miles from Dodge City, and the idea hit me that maybe I could get a job as an Army scout. I got it easily enough and spent the next three years bouncing around between one Army post and another, from Fort Yuma in New Mexico to Fort Laramie.

In spite of trying to forget Jennie, I was never able to. I thought about her a lot. She was like most folks on the frontier, I decided. She didn't even think Indians were human. She thought of them as animals, as savage wild animals whose only instinct was to kill. And she figured that because I'd been with them so long, I was as wild as they were. My killing the Comanches that captured her and later the white men who tried to steal her herd only proved her point.

I kept telling myself that she wasn't for me. She had probably remarried and had more kids by her new man. I'd probably never see her again. That was what I kept telling myself.

But I never quite got her face out of my dreams. I never quite accepted the idea that I'd never see her again.

I heard Dr. Porter yelling at Captain Benteen. His face was red and covered with sweat and dust. His hands were bloody and so was his uniform. He looked harassed and desperate.

Benteen hurried to him and the surgeon gestured toward the pile of empty canteens. He pointed to his wounded, laid out in neat lines upon the bloody, rain-soaked ground. It was plain that he was telling Benteen that his wounded needed water if they were going to survive. But how in the hell were we going to get water for them? It was broad daylight. The Sioux might have temporarily withdrawn from the slope but they weren't far away.

I raised up and stared at the valley and at the

river, so tantalizingly close. I was desperately thirsty myself, both because of the fever from my wounds and because of loss of blood.

There was a ravine snaking toward the valley on the left side of our defense perimeter, a deep ravine that, even though it grew shallower when it reached the valley floor, continued nearly all the way to the river. A few men just might be able to work their way down the ravine, carrying canteens. Their chance of surviving and getting back was slim but it was a chance. In any event, without water a lot of the wounded were going to die.

I turned and looked at Payne, wondering why I could never learn to keep my damn mouth shut. "Lieutenant, a few men might be able to work down that ravine. If they kept low . . ."

He turned his head and stared at the ravine and at the river beyond. Rain was falling on the river now; wind was whipping the trees along its bank.

Payne shook his head. "You're crazy. It would be suicide."

I said, "We're going to be here at least today and tonight. A lot of the wounded are going to die if we don't get water for them."

He shook his head. I said, "Talk to Benteen

about it, Lieutenant. I'll go along. Ten men ought to be able to carry enough water to hold us for another day."

Payne nodded reluctantly and got to his feet. He crossed the compound to the surgeon and Benteen. He began to talk. Major Reno joined the group and the four talked earnestly for several minutes more.

At last Payne came back to me. He nodded. "We'll get some volunteers. Benteen said it was worth a try."

I got up out of the trench and walked toward the center of the compound and the pile of empty canteens. I heard Payne calling for volunteers. Other officers were also calling for volunteers from their respective troops. Benteen saw me and said, "Not you, Lorette. You've already got two wounds."

I said, "I'm going, Captain. They won't make it if I don't."

"What about your wounds?"

"They feel better now and the surgeon can give me some more morphine."

Benteen nodded at the surgeon, who brought me some of the powdered drug. He also brought me a sip of water with which to wash it down.

About a dozen men had gathered. They all looked scared but they looked determined too. Captain Benteen said, "Lorette is going along with you. You are each to take twelve canteens. Good luck."

The men nodded. A couple saluted perfunctorily. All of them suddenly looked as if they wished they had not volunteered.

I said, "Get your canteens. Hang six on each side. We'll go to the back side of the knoll and slip over into the ravine, one at a time. The first ones down are to wait until everybody is in the ravine."

I led the way to the back side of the knoll. The first man went down the slope quickly, sliding when he plunged into the ravine. The rain had dampened the ground, so there would be no dust to give us away.

The second man went down. I stared across the ravine at the slope beyond. The third man went down. As he did, I saw an Indian watching from behind a thick clump of brush. As the fourth man went down, the Sioux got up and, crouching as he ran, retreated swiftly toward the next ravine.

I knelt. The range was close to three hundred yards, but I didn't dare to miss. I fired and saw mud kick up just behind the running Indian.

I raised my sights and fired again. This time the buck went down, but he wasn't dead. He continued to crawl toward the shelter of the next ravine.

I drew a careful bead. Resting my left arm on my knee to steady it, I held my breath and fired.

The Indian was flung forward, face down, to the ground. Spread out, he laid still.

All the troopers were now in the ravine. I continued to scan the slope carefully to see if we had been observed by other Indians.

Down in the ravine, one of the men called, "Lorette, for God's sake come on! We haven't got all day."

I slid into the ravine. The morphine the surgeon had given me was beginning to take effect. My head felt light, as if it might float away. The pain in my side and shoulder was less, and I couldn't even feel the warmth of blood in the bandages.

For a while we were able to travel along the ravine erect, but before we had gone two hundred yards it began to grow shallower. The men were forced to stoop to stay concealed.

Ahead, the ravine made a turn sharp enough so that beyond the turn it was hidden from our view.

I realized that if there was going to be an ambush it would be waiting for us beyond that turn.

I called to the sergeant leading the group. He stopped until I caught up. I pointed ahead. "There could be trouble beyond that bend. Let me go ahead and look."

He nodded and I crept on carefully. My rifle held seven shots, of which I had expended three. I wished there was time to reload, but there was not.

Fortunately, a few shots in this ravine weren't likely to attract attention from above. Too many shots were being fired haphazardly for a few more to be noticed.

I came around the bend in the ravine. There were half a dozen Sioux waiting there for us. A rifle exploded almost in my face. The bullet missed but the cloud of powdersmoke temporarily blinded me.

I fired instantly without bothering to raise the gun. An arrow zipped past my head, striking one of the troopers who had just come into view behind.

He howled. I dropped instantly to the ground so that the troopers could shoot over me. I heard the sergeant shout, "Pick yer targets, boys. Them are single shot guns yer carryin'."

From the ground, I fired a second time, and saw one of the Sioux bucks grab his gushing throat. A volley blasted behind me, momentarily deafening. The sergeant leaped over me, rifle clubbed, and smashed the skull of the last remaining Indian.

I got up. I hadn't been hit and I wasn't hurt. I said, "Take a minute, Sergeant, and let the men reload." I was kneeling, busy reloading my Spencer.

The sergeant said, "Reload, all of you. Lively now!"

The men obeyed. There wasn't a pair of steady hands in the lot, but neither did there appear to be any who wanted to go back. One of the troopers had an arrow in his leg. He sat down and tried to pull it out, without success. The sergeant said, "Leave it in, man, leave it in. I'll break off the shaft for you, but if you pull it out you may not be able to get back." He went to the man, knelt and carefully broke off the shaft so that it was less than six inches long. The man's face got white but he didn't faint.

"Let's get on with it," the sergeant said and we continued down the ravine.

It was now less than three feet deep. No longer did we dare travel it on our feet. The troopers got down on hands and knees and crawled, the canteens dragging awkwardly.

The ground was muddy and very slick. Mud covered our hands to the extent that operating a rifle would be difficult should it be necessary. The sergeant raised a hand and the troopers halted, strung out in a line at least fifty feet long.

I raised up carefully behind a clump of sagebrush. The ravine was now little more than a gully. Indians seemed to be coming and going aimlessly across the valley floor. There were a few behind brush clumps, firing toward the horseshoe on the knoll. It was still raining lightly and there was a light, cool breeze. There was no longer a dust cloud in the valley but there was a blue haze of smoke.

A group of mounted Indians was riding toward us, still a quarter mile away. I ducked back. "Let's get moving. There are twenty or thirty of them riding straight toward us."

The sergeant waved an arm at the men behind. We crawled on as swiftly as we could. Less than a hundred yards farther on we were forced to drop to our bellies to stay concealed.

I kept glancing behind uneasily. If we were discovered now, it would be slaughter. Not a one of
us would get back alive. Prone in the gully, with
hands too muddy to operate a rifle effectively,
we'd be sitting ducks for the Sioux.

I saw a group I had spotted earlier cross the
ravine several hundred yards behind. Not a one of
them looked toward me. They seemed intent on
watching the knoll where the bulk of the command remained. One of this group wore a hat that
looked like the one Mitch Bouyer had worn.
Behind me the sergeant whispered, "That's
Bouyer's hat."

Bouyer had gone with Custer. If he was dead,
it was probable that Custer was also dead, but
even yet we could not be absolutely sure. Custer
might have retreated into the hills as we had done.
He might be alive and fighting back . . .

The river was now less than two hundred yards
away. Short of it by forty or fifty feet, the gully leveled out. We'd have to make a run for it and hope
we weren't seen.

I crawled on. When I reached the place where
the ravine leveled out I glanced at the sergeant
immediately behind. "If we make a run for it one
at a time there'll be less chance of being noticed

than if we all go in a group."

He nodded. "You go first, Lorette. The sight of that water must be drivin' you damn near out of your mind. Get yourself a good long drink while I hold the men here. When you signal, I'll send the first one in."

I nodded, licking my cracked, dry lips. I had almost forgotten that we were surrounded by hostile Sioux. I had almost reached the point where the thought of that clear cool water drove everything else out of my mind.

I got to my feet and sprinted for the river. There was a break in its steep bank, a cut made by water rushing down the ravine. I scrambled down that cut, crossed a rocky little beach and flung myself face down at the riverbank.

I put my face into the water, sucking it up as noisily as any horse. I drank as much as I dared, then rolled, sat up and looked toward the men still waiting in the ravine. I crept to the cut in the riverbank and raised up enough to see the sergeant and the men. I waved carefully.

The first of the men got up and sprinted toward me. He came plunging down through the cut in the bank. Immediately he shed the canteens and flopped beside the river to get himself a drink.

I began to fill canteens. There wasn't much use now in worrying about the Indians. If they discovered us they'd kill every one of us. The thing for us to do was to fill the canteens as quickly as possible and get the hell out of here.

XVIII

ONE BY ONE, the men sprinted into the stream bed and flopped on the riverbank to drink. Afterward, each began filling his canteens.

It took a little time. Each canteen had to be held beneath the surface while water entered and air bubbled out. I finished filling mine, slung them over my shoulders, picked up my rifle and climbed the bank high enough to see the valley floor.

We had not, apparently, been noticed yet. I began to feel encouraged about our chances of getting back. Behind me the men were not talking but there was a confusion of scuffing and splashing as they continued hastily to fill canteens.

I called, "Easy. Take your time. None of them have spotted us."

Suddenly from behind a clump of trees downstream about a dozen Sioux came into sight riding straight toward me. I called softly, "Get your guns ready. We're about to have visitors."

Immediately there was a scrambling and an increased splashing from behind. The men slung their canteens awkwardly and crept up beside me, guns ready in their hands. The sergeant growled, "Hold your fire. Maybe they'll go by."

The group of painted horsemen drew near. They were now less than fifty feet away. Suddenly the man next to me sneezed.

The sergeant cursed. Immediately he bawled, "Fire!" and the volley rang out. Four of the Sioux horses galloped away riderless. The remaining Indians stared toward us unbelievingly.

I was firing my Spencer as fast as I could take aim. The troopers were desperately trying to reload. I knocked down three of the Sioux with four shots before the troopers' second volley banged out raggedly.

Three Sioux remained. They turned and galloped away. I managed to get one of them before they got out of range. He fell from his horse and lay twitching on the ground.

The sergeant yelled, "Let's go! Them two will be back with a hundred before you can say Jack Robinson."

He leaped out of the river bottom and sprinted for the shallow ravine. He ran recklessly until he was well into it.

The others followed. I had intended to bring up the rear but a corporal said, "Go on, Lorette. I'll come last."

I didn't argue with him. Instinctively bending low, I ran to the ravine. The others were crawling along it ahead of me. As soon as they could, they got off their knees and ran, crouching low so that they would not be seen.

I could not yet hear the rumble of galloping horses' hoofs but I could hear Indians in the distance yelling unintelligibly. The corporal came up the ravine behind me, canteens banging against each other and against his running legs. He called urgently to the men ahead, "Get going up there. We ain't got all day!"

Ahead of me a man snarled something over his shoulder at the corporal. I thought this was a hell of a place to get caught. The Sioux could fire down at us. They could close the ravine both ahead of us and behind. They could trap us and wipe us out.

The others seemed to have the same idea. Each man crowded the one ahead, cursing angrily, trying to hurry him.

It had to happen. I had known it would happen when the two Sioux got away. Above us and on both sides, mounted Indians suddenly appeared. Only a couple or three had guns but the others had arrows and tomahawks. The man ahead of me went down, blood streaming from a tomahawk wound on the side of his head. I helped him up. His eyes were dazed and uncomprehending. I yelled into his ear, "Get going, damn it! You're not hurt that bad!"

He nodded dumbly and stumbled on. I stopped long enough to fire at one of the Sioux that had a gun. His horse shied away from the muzzle blast. Horse and rider disappeared from my view.

No longer was there any reason for trying to stay concealed. Straightening, the men scrambled recklessly along the steep ravine. Their guns were empty but there was no time to reload.

My Spencer was empty too. I heard an arrow thud into the body of the corporal in back of me.

I whirled.

He was down on one knee, shaking his head like a wounded buffalo. I yanked him to his feet. The arrow was in the muscles of his back, protruding at an angle. I pushed him ahead of me.

From above us cavalry carbines roared unexpectedly. I suddenly realized how deep the ravine had become, realized that we were immediately below the knoll.

The first of the men were already climbing out. A couple of dozen troopers slid down into the ravine to help the wounded out. A ragged cheer raised from the men waiting on the knoll.

The Sioux withdrew. I reached the barricade and was helped over. I went to the center of the compound and began shedding my canteens.

My head was whirling. I felt weak and my knees felt as though they would collapse. The breeze was stronger now and it had stopped raining. The sun made a luminous ball behind the thinning clouds.

Lieutenant Payne was beside me, supporting me. "Miles, you had better lie down before you fall."

I nodded weakly. I sat down and laid back against a pile of medical supplies. I closed my eyes. Payne asked, "Miles can you hear me?"

I nodded, my eyes still closed. Payne said excitedly, "Reno is going to recommend every one of you for a Medal of Honor."

I didn't bother to point out that they don't award the Medal of Honor to civilians. My head was whirling. And suddenly I was asleep. The morphine had finally taken full effect.

I did not awake until midafternoon, but when I did, I felt better than at any time since receiving the wounds in my shoulder and along my ribs. There was a certain grogginess about the way I felt that I supposed was because of the morphine.

And I was hungry. I was ravenous. Firing had slackened until it had almost stopped. Occasionally a rifle would bang away on some nearby hill and the bullet would strike the knoll and ricochet away. Otherwise everything seemed unnaturally still.

Men were sleeping everywhere. Others, unshaven and grimy-faced, stared out across the valley of the Little Big Horn with stubborn patience, waiting for the next development.

I sat up. The surgeon saw me and brought me a cup of water. I drank it. "Is there anything to eat?"

He nodded, left, and a few minutes later a trooper brought me a bowl of soup. It tasted like beef but I supposed it was horsemeat soup. The man gave me a piece of hardtack to eat with it.

I sipped the soup. It was very hot. I thought of Jennie and for the first time since yesterday morning I began to believe I might see her again. Apparently the Sioux had given up trying to annihilate us. Apparently the cost of doing so had discouraged them.

It didn't matter whether Custer was dead or not. Terry and Gibbon were somewhere north of here. Crook was somewhere to the south. Eventually one of their commands would locate us. Or the Indians would withdraw. Either way we would be safe.

I finished the soup and hardtack and put the cup down on the ground. I stood up carefully.

My head reeled and I felt myself swaying. I waited out the weakness and at last my head began to clear.

I walked toward the trench where A Troop was. Payne saw me coming and grinned at me. Glancing up the trench I saw Private Overby. He looked at me impassively. He must believe, as we all did, that Custer was dead, but he didn't seem elated. He didn't seem to be feeling anything but weariness.

I said, "I saw an Indian wearing Mitch Bouyer's hat."

Payne nodded. He stared out into the valley. The rain had stopped before I went to sleep. While I was sleeping the breeze had dried the ground. A galloping Sioux half a mile away raised a plume of dust. Payne said, "Take a good look, Miles. That's the biggest Indian gathering a white man's ever seen. I'll bet it's the biggest that will ever be seen. They've whipped us but they'll live to regret it. Custer was a hero to the American people, whatever he was to the rest of us. They won't take his death lightly. They'll want revenge."

I nodded. I'd suffered considerably at the hands of Indians, but in spite of it, I couldn't help feeling sad. They were a proud, free race. Now they would be hunted, hounded, killed or enslaved, until none were left or until they were confined like animals. Payne asked, "What do you think they'll do?"

"They'll leave. They're not afraid of Terry or of Crook but they'll leave because they're tired of fighting us. Maybe they'll scatter, maybe not. But they'll leave."

"And then what?"

I didn't know. I said, "Some will go into Canada where the Army can't follow, I suppose. Some will slip back to the reservation. A few will probably stay out here."

"You don't think they'll attack again?"

"I doubt it."

"And what will you do?"

"I'll go back to Dodge," I said.

It seemed strange to be thinking in terms of living, in terms of going back to Dodge. Because once before I'd returned to Dodge, in the spring of '73. I hadn't figured there was much chance of persuading Jennie to marry me but I knew I had to try. I was damned if I was going to lose her by default.

She wasn't at the hotel but then I hadn't expected her to be. I inquired about her and they told me she had a ranch north of Dodge a ways. They told me how to get to it and I asked if she was married again and they said no.

I rode out, getting more nervous and excited all the time. Her ranch was in a little draw where there was clear water and a lot of cottonwoods. I rode in and knocked on the kitchen door and she answered it, with soapsuds on her arms clear to her elbows and brushing a little wisp of hair out of her eyes with the back of her hand. I could hear the two kids yelling and playing down at the barn.

I'd almost forgotten how she looked. I'd forgotten but I'd remembered too. I'd remembered the strong, clean lines of her face even if I had forgotten the color of her eyes. She wasn't as thin as I remembered her. She had on a fresh print dress and she looked so good I just stood there staring at her while she stared back at me as if she'd forgotten all the nasty things she had ever said to me. Her voice quivered as she said, "Miles! Oh Miles, come in!"

I went in and brushed against her and suddenly she was in my arms and I was holding her as if I'd never let her go and she was holding on to me like she didn't want me to. It was like a prairie fire and there weren't any questions in either one of us. It was like this had been meant to be from the very first time I'd set eyes on her.

Well, we hitched up her buckboard and drove into Dodge that same night and were married and she left the two children with a woman in town and we went back out to her ranch alone. It was like we'd been hungering and starving for each other all our lives. It was like nothing I've ever experienced. I didn't know being with a woman could be like it was with her.

We spent a week together out there alone and then we drove in to Dodge and picked her children up.

Things kind of settled down for a while after that. I took over working her ranch and she sure had needed somebody to do that. There were calves a year old that didn't have a brand on them. I worked hard and we had two good years and two more kids, both boys. But it was too good to last. In the spring of 1875 a bunch of Cheyenne rebelled against the government putting irons on their chiefs and shipping them off to Florida. They broke out of their reservation and trailed north, passing within thirty miles of our place. I was on spring roundup and a bunch of raiding bucks found Jennie and the kids alone. When I got back the house was burned, the kids were dead, and Jennie had been raped a couple of times by every buck in the raiding party and left for dead.

She screamed when she saw me. She screamed and screamed and kept on screaming until finally I had to hit her with my fist and knock her out. I put her in the buckboard and drove her in to Dodge. I left her in the care of the doctor and a woman who knew her and got on my horse to ride after the Cheyenne.

I picked up their tracks easily enough. They headed north and west and finally joined up with the tracks of the main band. That didn't bother me because I knew the track of every horse in the raiding party. I knew each crack and broken place in each hoof and when I found those horses I'd recognize them.

The Army reached the Cheyenne before I did, though, on Sappa Creek, and there was damn little left when I got there. The lodges and supplies had been burned, the bodies thrown up on the pile to burn along with them. The horses had been shot but in spite of the stench, I went among them and found the ones I had been following. I knew that now I'd never find out whether the bucks that had burned our place were dead or not.

I went back to Dodge. When Jennie saw me she began to scream again as if I was one of the bucks that had hurt her so.

The doctor said she was hopelessly insane because of what had happened and that she'd have to go to an asylum for the insane. I said no, she wasn't going to any asylum as long as I was alive. I got Mrs. McGinnis, the woman who had been

taking care of Jennie, to continue doing it, and I
got them a house at the edge of town where they
could be by themselves. I stayed around long
enough to dispose of the ranch and cattle. I put
the money in the bank and told the banker to give
them as much as they needed to live on.

I knew Jennie wasn't insane. As long as she
didn't see me or have any more trouble with
Indians, she'd eventually be all right. In spite of us
being married and together those two years, she
still thought of me as Indian, and wild, even if
she'd managed to tame me temporarily. I guess
she'd just been hurt too much by Indians to ever
get over it or forgive them for it and she couldn't
forget I had been one of them.

I went to Wichita and tried to forget what had
happened by staying drunk. I got into a lot of
fights and once damn near killed a man. I woke up
in jail. It was coming on spring by the time I got
out and I heard the Army was going after the
Sioux as soon as there was grass so I made up my
mind I'd go along. The things that had happened
to Jennie, and the years I'd lived with the whites
and scouted for the Army, had kind of turned me
against the Indians anyway. Maybe I had some
idea that when they were all penned up on reser-

vations or dead, things like what had happened to Jennie couldn't happen any more.

I signed on as scout at Fort Abraham Lincoln, but since they weren't going to leave for about four weeks, I rode back down to Kansas to see how Jennie was, about as mixed up in my mind as anyone could be. I hated Custer for what he had done at the Washita. I had begun to hate the Cheyenne for what they'd done to Jennie, and I hated the Comanches for what they'd done to her earlier. I still didn't know whether I'd end up living with the Indians or with the whites and I wasn't sure I wanted to live with either one.

I sent a message out to Mrs. McGinnis that I wanted to see her at the hotel. I didn't want to hurt Jennie by scaring her.

Mrs. McGinnis came to the hotel and we sat in the lobby and talked. I asked her how Jennie was and she said all right, except that she wept a lot, just quiet weeping with tears running down her cheeks and dropping into her lap. She said Jennie wasn't going to get any better unless something happened to change things and she thought I ought to come out and see if I couldn't talk to her. She thought Jennie was weeping for me as much as for the children and that Jennie needed me whether she knew it or not. I told her I'd signed up to go on the spring campaign against the Sioux and that I couldn't stay even if Jennie wanted me, but she thought I ought to see Jennie before I left.

I've never been more scared in my life than I was during that walk out to where Jennie and Mrs. McGinnis lived. I was scared she'd look at me and start screaming again. I knew if she did I'd go away and never come back. I'd never see her again. Mrs. McGinnis went in first to talk to her so that seeing me wouldn't come as such a shock. After a few minutes she called me to come in.

I went in, my hat in my hand, wishing my skin wasn't so dark from the sun, wishing my hair wasn't so long, wishing I'd got me a store bought suit to wear instead of what I had on. Jennie was paler than I remembered her. She was thinner too. But she was the most beautiful thing I'd ever seen. She looked at me, and her face twisted as if she'd felt a sudden pain somewhere. Tears filled her eyes and her lips began to quiver. She held out her arms to me and said just one word: "Miles!"

Mrs. McGinnis had disappeared. I went over to Jennie's chair and got down on my knees in front of her and put my arms around her. She held to me the way she had that day we were married so long ago and her whole body shook like she had a chill.

I didn't say anything about the past. I just stayed with her for a whole week until I had to leave for Fort Abraham Lincoln to report. She wept when I left, but she was smiling too and the last words she said to me were, "Come back to me, Miles! I'm going to be all right now. I am going to be a wife to you again."

I realized suddenly that I could have been with Custer yesterday as easily as with Reno. I could have been killed in the grove or in any of a dozen other places since the 7th attacked the Sioux. But I hadn't been killed. It was like something or someone was guarding me so that I could go back to Jennie and take care of her, so that she'd never again slip away into that terrible world where she'd gone after her children were killed by the Cheyenne.

XIX

NOT SINCE I had looked down from the Crow's Nest at the monstrous Sioux pony herd had I actually believed I was going to get out of the Little Big Horn valley alive.

Now I realized that Jennie and I could have a ranch again, a place where we could be alone, where we could raise children undisturbed. Not again would Indians raid across the plains. The defeat of the 7th Cavalry would accomplish what no victory could. It would ensure the eventual defeat of the Indians. It would unite all the dissenting white voices into one determined voice.

I stared out across the wide valley. Indians still galloped back and forth. I saw a plume of smoke rise in the distance, another, a third.

I touched Lieutenant Payne's shoulder. "Look. They're firing the grass."

"That means they're pulling out for sure."

"Yes."

Others had seen what we had seen and had

interpreted it as we had. A ragged cheer rose from the weary men, from those still able to cheer.

I realized suddenly that I had not heard a rifle shot for ten minutes or more. It was over. It was over and I was alive.

Out of the north the smoke clouds boiled. The grass, while dry enough to burn, was still wet enough to send great clouds of bluish smoke into the air. The wind was strong enough to drive the smoke ahead of the flames across the valley floor.

There were times when we seemed to be looking down upon a bank of cloud or fog. At other times, the wind would shift momentarily, allowing us a glimpse of the vast Sioux village and the horsemen galloping, with what seemed like aimless confusion, back and forth.

Behind me the wounded moaned. The surgeon and the troopers helping him worked unceasingly. The men who had slept now wakened and relieved those who had stayed awake.

Minutes dragged into hours. The sun, sometimes visible through clouds as a luminous ball, slowly settled in the western sky.

I laid back against the bank of the trench and closed my eyes. I could see Jennie's face now, her eyes glistening with moisture, her smile hesitant and tremulous. Wind had parted the curtain of smoke. The tipis were coming down, one by one. The village was slowly disappearing before our eyes.

We ate cold rations, this night, because there was no wood with which to build fires. And at seven, the first of the Sioux travois passed in front of us.

Was this some cruel trick, I wondered, some gigantic hoax? Was it a plan to deceive us into thinking they were leaving the valley of the Little Big Horn? Did they intend to sweep in to the attack as soon as we left the safety of our dug-in position on the knoll?

I didn't think so. Not for several hours had the Sioux showed the slightest interest in us.

I stared down the valley toward the north, trying to penetrate the smoke, trying to see if Terry and Gibbon were coming up the Little Big Horn, but the smoke was too thick. Besides, I doubted if they would be close enough to see, even if the air was clear.

The men remaining to the battered 7th Cavalry stood in their trenches to watch the gigantic, slowly moving column of Sioux. It all but defied description as it gained size and momentum passing in front of us.

It had started with but a single travois moving south toward the headwaters of the Little Big Horn but as the movement gained momentum, the column widened like a gigantic wedge. A quarter mile back from that first travois, it was half a mile in width. It continued to widen as more and more tipis came down, as more and more families finished loading their possessions upon travois and began to follow the others south.

Beside me, Lieutenant Payne uttered an exclamation of awe. "Holy Jesus Christ, look at that!"

I turned my face and grinned. "It's something, isn't it?" And it was. The column of Sioux could now be seen in its entirety. It was three miles long, more than a mile wide at its widest point. It contained thousands upon thousands of horses dragging travois behind. Thousands upon thousands of painted, befeathered horsemen accompanied the travois. More thousands of loose horses traveled along the edges of the column and in the rear, herded along by half naked boys on barebacked mounts.

They did not even look toward us in their victorious arrogance. They paid no attention to us at all. The Sioux suddenly reminded me of an ancient buffalo bull, who has been beset by wolves but who has driven them away, who retreats from the field of battle with lofty dignity.

The countless thousands of travois poles raised a cloud of dust dwarfing anything we had seen before. It lifted higher and higher until it concealed the hills and ridges to the south and west, until it blotted out what was showing of the sun, until it filled our nostrils and made us cough.

Patient and seemingly endless, the column crawled deliberately past, climbing the gentle valley grade toward the headwaters of the Little Big Horn far to the south of us. It took a couple of hours to pass. As the last of it straggled past our position on the knoll, the sky was growing dark.

In numbed exhaustion, the men laid down and slept. The sky cleared and the stars shone down. The dust slowly settled out of the air and the smoke from the smoldering grass fires drifted away on the breeze.

Sentries walked their posts inside the compound, occasionally calling out, giving their post numbers and the word that all was well. The others slept, some snoring loudly with utter weariness. I also slept, a fever-ridden, uneasy sleep because of the wounds I had sustained.

I awoke as dawn began to gray the eastern sky. Feeling stronger than at any time since being wounded, I got up stiffly and walked to the only fire burning within the perimeter of our defense.

There was a blackened pot of coffee on the coals. I got a cup and poured it full.

Reno and Benteen came to the fire and stared down at me. "Do you think you could make a scout out there?" Reno asked, "Do you think you could find out what happened to the general?"

I nodded.

The two hesitated, but at last Reno said, "If he's . . . well, if he and his men are dead, I'd like to have you ride north until you locate General Terry. I'd like to have you lead him here. The Indians seem to have left the valley but we can't be sure. They may have withdrawn in the hope of luring us off this hill."

I nodded again, sipping the scalding coffee gratefully. I wasn't afraid of going out on scout. I figured the Sioux had left the valley for good. They were miles away by now, probably after traveling throughout the night. They knew Terry was on his way. Their scouts had probably told them exactly where he was. That explained their leaving, moving their entire encampment out of the valley so unexpectedly.

I finished the coffee and put down the cup. I fumbled my way to the picket line.

There was a faint line of gray in the east. I managed to locate my horse, which I had left with the pack train day before yesterday. I saddled him and led him back to the fire. Here I checked the loads in my Spencer carbine and those in my revolver.

I realized that I had been anxious for this all along. I wanted to know what had happened to the general. I suppose I knew that he was dead, that all the men with him were also dead, but I wanted to see it with my own two eyes.

I swung to the horse's back. The line of gray in the east was plainer now. I knew the main body of Sioux had left and I was satisfied they were planning no ambush in case Reno's remaining men left the knoll. But I was also aware that Sioux scouts might still be lurking in the area. Crazy Horse and Gall and Sitting Bull would want to know where Terry was, where Gibbon was, where Crook was, every minute of the time.

Watchfully I left the knoll by the open end of the horseshoe. I stayed in a ravine, heading for the valley floor.

It was good to be mounted again. There was still pain in my shoulder and in my side and I still had some fever but I'd had wounds before and I knew I was on the mend.

I reached the level of the valley floor and rode along the fringe of bluffs facing it. Custer had taken his men into the rough country on my right. His last known position would be due north of where I was right now.

I had never been in this area before, but from maps I knew there was a small creek ahead called Medicine Tail Creek. Most of the year it was dry, I had been told. Now, in early summer, it probably contained a trickle of water at least.

Custer had probably crossed Medicine Tail Creek and gone beyond. How far, I had no idea.

The whole sky now was gray. I stopped my horse and stared around warily. I had come through the battle, through the siege that followed it. I had come through several scouts and had survived my pursuit of Nick Stavola. I was damned if I was going to get myself killed now because I didn't have sense enough to keep my eyes peeled.

Nothing moved in the Little Big Horn valley but a crippled horse. Nothing moved on the bluffs.

I reined my horse right and climbed through the sagebrush covered hills. Bearing steadily right, I finally crossed a wide trail of shod hoofprints that could only have been made by Custer's men.

Pink touched the eastern sky, pink that turned to orange and at last to gold. The sun came up, a brassy ball shining none too brightly through the haze of dust lying close to the ground. The trail I followed was wide and broad, easy to follow and hard to lose in spite of the fact that the unshod prints of many Sioux horses had almost obliterated it in spots.

I realized suddenly that my hands were trembling. My knees had tremors in them. There was a cold chill running along my spine. What would I find at the end of the trail I was following? Would I find Custer, dug in as Benteen and Reno were? Or would I find stripped and mutilated bodies lying scattered like broken dolls?

A breeze blew out of the north, straight into my face. As the light strengthened in the sky, it stiffened into a steady wind. By the time the sun came up it was whipping my horse's tail and mane.

He raised his head, ears pricking forward. He smelled something, I thought. He balked, tossing his head, trying to turn aside. I dug heels into his sides and tightened the reins, forcing him to go on.

Something fluttered along the ground in front of me, catching my eye, drawing my glance. My horse shied violently. Suddenly there were fluttering bits of paper all around. Green paper. Money.

I had a strange compulsion to dismount and gather them up. It was a normally thrifty impulse that was difficult to resist. But I did resist it and forced the horse to continue.

The money belonged to Custer's troopers, who had been paid just outside of Bismarck en route here. It was one thing for which the Sioux had no use.

I was certain, now, what I would find ahead of me. Custer and all his men were dead. No longer could there be any doubt.

XX

THE BED of Medicine Tail Creek was littered with currency. I rode along its bottom, following the well beaten trail left by Custer's five company command.

On my left, the bank rose higher and higher. Custer had probably been made uneasy by its height, knowing how devastating Sioux fire from its crest could be, because shortly the trail angled right and began to climb out to higher ground.

The trail of six or seven horses, however, continued down the nearly dry creek bed. A patrol, I supposed, sent to scout the Little Big Horn and look for a ford.

The river was about four or five hundred yards away but I followed the trail and put my horse into the river at the point where the trail disappeared. The animal climbed out on the other side, ears pricked toward a patch of heavy brush on my right.

I rode that way. I rounded a high clump of

brush and pulled my horse to a sudden halt. Half
a dozen bodies lay sprawled ahead of me, starkly
white and naked, some with streaks of dried blood
on them. Custer's patrol had found their ford but
they hadn't been able to return and so report.

I rode closer. I recognized Lieutenant Harrington. I recognized three of the others, thought
I didn't know their names. I turned and rode back
across the river and climbed out.

I stopped a moment, my body feeling strangely
cold. I had known Harrington fairly well. I could
almost see him riding down this ravine heading
toward the river, his men clattering along behind.
The Sioux probably had not yet massed when he
crossed, but they had trapped him there, coming
up on all sides of him. There had been hundreds,
I supposed, against the handful with Harrington.
It must have been over in seconds, or in minutes
at the most. Harrington and those with him had
never had a chance.

Growing progressively colder as I rode, I put
my horse up the right bank of Medicine Tail Creek
at an oblique, following the deeply pounded trail.

At the lip of it, a part of the trail bore right, and
here the shod prints of the cavalry horses were
sometimes obliterated by the unshod prints of the

ponies belonging to the Sioux. I stopped my horse and stared at the surrounding area.

At this point, I guessed, the Sioux had made their first screeching attack. They had struck Custer's column in the center, almost breeching it, by their pressure forcing its center to the right.

I found the first scattering of bodies here, a man from C Company and farther to the right, two men from F. Beyond and more to my left, I found a man who had been attached to E.

Somewhere, unnoticed by me earlier, Keogh's I Troop and Calhoun's L must have been detached, perhaps to remain in reserve. Or else I and L troops had just been lucky so far in not losing any men.

Continuing, I saw that Custer had tried to form a line at the crest of a little ridge, with E Troop on the left, C in the center, and F on the right. More bodies were scattered haphazardly along the ridge.

The pressure of the attacking Sioux must have been terrible. Thousands of their hoof prints in places all but obliterated the trail of Custer's three companies. More bodies lay naked and white, staring at the sky. The trail of E Company kept bearing farther left, forced that way by the relentless pressure of the Sioux.

I closed my eyes. I could almost hear the shrieks of the Indians, the shouts of Custer's officers. The dust of battle and the powdersmoke seemed real in my nostrils. Here, I supposed, Custer and his captains must have begun to realize that the 7th faced annihilation by the Sioux. Here they must have looked squarely at death for the first time since the campaign began.

And there was more money here, scattered, fluttering along the ground, lodged in clumps of sagebrush everywhere. Two hundred and twenty-five men had been with Custer. Each had been carrying a month's pay at least. It added up to several thousand dollars in currency. No wonder so much was scattered everywhere.

E Company had continued, apparently now cut off from the rest of the command. The number of unshod hoof prints in the ground testified to the overwhelming force that had thrown itself against them. E Troop had left a trail of stripped and mutilated bodies in its wake. Forced up against the lip of still another deep ravine, E had turned right along the edge of it. I found Lieutenant Sturgis lying here.

On up the ridge the trail continued, marked by

bodies scattered everywhere. I felt now as if there was icewater in my veins. I had seen death before, but never anything as devastating and complete as this. I counted twenty-seven bodies along the lip of that ravine. One of the last was that of Captain Smith. Beyond was nothing, until I encountered the trail of C Company on slightly higher ground.

From here I stared toward the river once again. Back in the direction I had come and closer to the river, I saw another body lying by itself. Curiously I rode to it even though it was several hundred yards away. It was Mitch Bouyer. There was a gaping wound in one hip. There were other wounds in Bouyer's chest. I stared at him, wanting to get down and bury him decently but knowing I had no time.

I could imagine what had happened to Bouyer because I knew the man's character. He'd lost his temper when the Sioux began killing troopers on all sides of him. He'd probably launched a one man charge that had carried him this far before they brought him down. I turned and rode back up the ridge, cutting the trail of C Company and following it reluctantly.

At the top of the ridge, I pulled my horse to a halt again. I didn't want to go on but I knew I must. I had completely forgotten that there still might be danger to me from Sioux scouts lurking in the area. Nothing around me moved, nothing but the brush, stirred by the wind, nothing but the endless, fluttering bits of currency.

Chilled thoroughly by now, I forced myself to go on. I had hated Custer. Once I had even wanted to kill him if I could. But suddenly I couldn't hate him any more. I could only feel pity for a man whose greed and ambition had driven him to this.

Pressed relentlessly, he had retreated along this ridge, with the mutilated remnants of Troops F and C. Tom Custer, his brother, had commanded C. Yates had commanded F, the gray horse troop.

Where had Keogh and Calhoun gone, I wondered curiously. Held in reserve, they must have been caught by nearly as many Indians as Custer's three troops had.

I followed the trail of bodies and dead horses up the ridge. I reached a little group, thirty or forty in all, but I didn't stop. I could come back to them, I told myself. Right now I wanted to know where Keogh and Calhoun were. I had to be sure that none of their troopers had survived.

Beyond the group of bodies I rode, toward the

upper end of the ridge. A single horse stood grazing a quarter mile away. I recognized the animal instantly. It was Comanche, Captain Keogh's horse.

I was now headed back toward the bed of Medicine Tail Creek. I found Keogh, his body surrounded by a few of his men, some of whom I recognized. Farther along the trail of scattered bodies, I found Calhoun. I kept going, by now almost numb with shock. The last time I had seen these men they had been alive. Now they were all dead.

I reached the edge of the ravine that held Medicine Tail Creek. I saw the body of Sergeant Butler of Calhoun's company lying alone on the slope. He must have been the first man killed, I thought, or else he had been sent to try and reach Reno or Benteen.

I turned around and headed back up the ridge. Off on one side of it, I saw five more bodies that I had not seen before. These were men from Keogh's company. One was named Porter. I could not recall what his rank had been.

I dug heels into my horse's sides. He broke into a steady lope. Occasionally he would prick his ears toward one of the bodies, or shy away.

I had never thought of myself as being sensi-
tive. I guess my stomach is as strong as anyone's.
But I felt like getting off my horse and vomiting. I
felt like I was going to be seeing these white and
naked bodies in nightmares for a long, long time
to come.

I reached the end of the ridge at last. Here the
group of thirty or more bodies lay. Most were
stripped but one was not. I got off my horse and
walked to where he lay.

It was Custer. His eyes were closed and there
was a peaceful expression on his face, as though
he had gone to sleep. There was a small, bluish
hole in his left temple, from which a little trickle
of blood had run and dried.

Strange, I thought, that his body had not been
touched. There were plenty of Indians that hated
him bitterly, both among the Sioux and among
the Cheyenne. Strange, unless he had, in those
last moments of agony, shot himself. If he had, it
would explain the fact that he had been neither
stripped nor mutilated. Indians look with awe and
fear upon one who has committed suicide.

I shook my head dazedly. Suicide would have
been unthinkable to Custer, whose courage no
one had ever questioned, whatever else they had

to say about the man. Unless his coming here, unless attacking countless thousands of Sioux with only two hundred and twenty-five could be considered a form of suicide.

Slow anger began stirring in my mind. It grew like the embers of a fire, fanned by a sudden wind. Damn him, I thought. Damn him to hell! He had never cared about his men. He had never considered them more than tools of his own ambition, to be used, dulled, sacrificed and thrown away.

He had thrown away two hundred and twenty-five good men here in the valley of the Little Big Horn, unthinking that each was a human being like himself, with a family whose members would grieve his death, with children, perhaps, who now must grow up fatherless.

There was an elusive smell to this place, the smell of blood and death. Staring down at Custer's face, I wondered what history would say of him. Would historians dare say that he had been a fool? Would they dare say that in his voracious greed for glory he had committed the ultimate in military folly, that of attacking an overwhelming superior force without reconnaissance, and that he had compounded his incredible folly by dividing his small force into four separate commands?

His greed had led him to betray Reno, to whom he had promised support. How could history say anything complimentary about a man like this?

It seemed indecent to leave the dead of the 7th lying this way but I had no choice. There was nothing I could do for them. I had orders to go on, to locate Terry and Gibbon and lead them back to the remnants of Reno's command.

I angled off the hill, leaving the scattered bodies behind. I headed down in the valley of the Little Big Horn, keeping a wary eye out for scouting Indians.

All those who had hated Custer had been revenged, I thought. The Washita was avenged and so were the executed troopers of Front Royal. The dead deserters, for whom Nick Stavola had wanted vengeance, also were revenged.

Occasionally now the sun shone down through a break in the spotty, puffy clouds drifting in the sky overhead, but I still felt cold. The land was black, where the Sioux had burned the grass.

I passed over the place where their villages had been. Discarded articles were strewn around, children's handmade toys, broken and useless now, household articles, bones and bits of hide. Here the grass was literally trampled into the ground. And there was the smell of habitation, of human excretions, of dogs, of rotting meat. A wolf slunk from a buffalo's leg bone and disappeared into the trees lining the river. Several coyotes ran for the hillside and disappeared into the high sagebrush there. I don't know how many miles I rode. But at last I saw horsemen coming toward me, not Indian horsemen but cavalrymen. I touched heels to my horse's sides and he broke into a trot. The gait made my wounds hurt but the sight of Custer and his dead had unnerved me, I suppose. I wanted someone to talk to. I wanted to look at a white and friendly face.

At the head of the scouts, Lieutenant Bradley rode. He galloped toward me. "Lorette! Thank God! Where is General Custer, man? Some of our Indian scouts told us he was dead with all his men."

I nodded. "He is."

"Good God!" He stared at me. "How did you survive?"

"I was with Reno and Benteen. They're dug in on a hill back there with about three hundred men."

Lieutenant Bradley turned his head and spoke

to one of his scouts, directing him to return to General Terry with the news. Then he turned to me. "I take it Custer is between Reno's command and here."

I nodded.

"Then we will go there and wait for General Terry to arrive. Major Reno is in no danger, is he?"

I said, "The Sioux have gone. They moved out during the night."

Bradley nodded. I turned my horse and he rode beside me. We headed toward the place where Custer lay. There was awe and unbelief on Bradley's face. He said, "It's unbelievable! How many men did Custer have with him?"

"Five troops. Two hundred and twenty-five, I suppose."

"For God's sake, how many Indians were here?"

"Five thousand. Ten. I don't know for sure. I do know that when they pulled out of this valley last night they made a column three miles long and more than a mile wide."

"Has anybody heard anything from General Crook?"

I shook my head.

For a long time we rode in silence. Bradley's face was pale, his eyes shocked. We reached the foot of the bluff upon which Custer lay with his men. I put my horse up the hill and Bradley followed me with his scouts.

Short of the bodies of E Troop's men by a hundred yards, we halted. Bradley stared, then turned his head and gave the orders for his scouts to dismount.

The scouts squatted silently on the ground. None showed any inclination to go closer and view the scattered bodies. Bradley said, "God! I can't believe it yet!" He turned his head and stared at me. "You're wounded."

I nodded. "The surgeon bandaged me."

"Has Reno lost many men?"

I nodded. "Fifty. A hundred. I don't know for sure."

"It must have been pure hell."

I grinned. "It was. I never saw so many goddam hostile Indians." I felt weak suddenly. I laid back on the ground and closed my eyes, holding onto my horse's reins.

I slept. When I awakened Terry's column was approaching. Terry dismounted and walked with his officers among the slain of Custer's command.

Terry's face was white with shock. There were tears in the eyes of some of his officers. They remounted quickly and I led them toward Reno's command on the hill.

Lieutenant Wallace and a handful of troopers rode down to meet us and to escort us back to the mauled command. Wallace looked at me and said one word, "Custer?"

"Back there, Lieutenant. Dead with all his men."

We reached the foot of the knoll. Looking toward its top I saw a line of bearded, grimy men staring down at us. Most of them were weeping unashamedly. A ragged cheer broke suddenly from their throats. Then all of them were yelling and waving their arms and pounding each other on the backs.

Terry himself had tears streaming down his cheeks as he dismounted in the center of the compound to take Reno's and Benteen's salutes. For ten minutes he listened to their emotional accounts of the battle and the subsequent siege. Then he said briskly, "We will camp in the valley beside the stream. Load your wounded into the ambulance wagons." He turned to one of his officers. "See to it that a meal is prepared immediately for these men. And we will need a large burial party at once."

I rode my horse to the general. "General, I'm not needed here. I'd like to be released."

"You're wounded, Mr. Lorette. Don't you want to go back with us? You can travel in one of the ambulances until you're well enough to ride."

I grinned faintly at him. "I've been riding, General. I don't need an ambulance."

"Where can we reach you in case there is an inquiry?"

"Dodge City, General. That's where I'll be."

Terry turned and looked at Reno and Benteen. "Is it all right with you if I let him go?"

Both men nodded. I leaned over and shook the major's hand. I shook Benteen's next. Benteen grinned at me, "Don't let those red devils get your hair, Lorette."

"No sir."

I looked at the exhausted troopers streaming on foot down off the knoll. I was reluctant to leave them. There was a bond between us now that neither time nor space could ever break.

But Jennie was waiting for me in Dodge. Turning my horse I rode away toward the south. I did not look back, and after a while there was only the vastness of earth and sky to keep me company.

But I was alive and suddenly my life seemed very, very sweet.

Center Point Publishing
600 Brooks Road ● PO Box 1
Thorndike ME 04986-0001 USA

(207) 568-3717

US & Canada:
1 800 929-9108